HOPE

George Hudoba

To my friends who endured my questions and nagging all these years. To Steve who was instrumental bringing a certain character to life...

Chapter One

The man was looking thru the double reinforced windows. Bellow him laid a city, a city on fire. Multiple grenades flew past the building, down the valley, straight into the heart of Akron. Past the city, where the naval base should have been a gigantic mushroom flew upwards, signaling the sad fact: this had become a nuclear war. It was the middle of the night, actually past midnight and the enemy was moving straight for the city. A man busted into the main atrium: "Sir, Calvin made it into the bank!"

"Is he back already?" The leader of the group turned around. He wore a crisp military dress, never hiding his true loyalties.

"Yes, sir! He hid the crystal in a safe place!"

"…And the documentation?"

"I gave Calvin some guidance papers to hide along with the item, but the rest are burned and destroyed!" The man reported and then asked candidly: "Are you sure it's necessary? I mean to sacrifice our lives?"

"John, it's a must! We have the antivirus and our friends in the AOCP (Alliance Of Central Planets) confirmed that it is working. They left two weeks ago and it's a shame we can't leave now on our own, but they," he nodded thru the windows, toward the city under siege "can't truly presume what's really happening out here in space! So yes, send our last transmission toward the SatCom relay system and activate the auto destruct!"

"Yes sir!" The man nodded and left.

The leader turned back toward the spectacular view, but suddenly an alarm went off. The man frowned and flipped couple switches on his table to see the nature of the disruption. He recognized the person banging on the outside door because he let out a curse walking away, toward the entrance.

"Officer, how can I help you, such a late time?" He forcibly smiled toward the police officer, who threw a paper at his face as he stormed in.

"Chief, you can't come in!" He gestured toward the returning John for help.

"Read it boss! I've got a search warrant!" The police officer turned around and faced him square on.

The man read the official paper, thought about it for a split second as he had no more, and after deciding the fate of the official, he nodded: "Be it Chief, it will be okay now! John?" He turned toward his second who scrutinized his superior's sudden change of heart toward the adversary:

"Sir, message is away and the countdown began! The staff is coming up to the atrium and we have about five minutes left!" He reported.

"Very well done John! The UNHL (United Nations of Humanlike Life-forms) and the Emperors will send our souls to heaven!" The group leader replied, sounding satisfied.

"Wait a minute! Who are the Emperors? What the hell is going on?" The police officer watched the man named John passing him. He did something with the door...

Alarmed, he shouted toward the man: "What are you doing?!"

"Well, you'll burn with us now, chief, no way out, no more hide and seek, no more threats! I am tired. Tired of you, tired of this wretched planet, tired that we did an excellent job, but our employers no longer need our help, tired that it became a waste of my and my valuable team's life!"

"What?" The police chief jumped to the door but it was locked, sealed tight with another door that had a numeric keypad.

The group leader smiled warmly: "No! You wanted in, because you were suspicious of us, of our doing! You'll know the truth, but you will not make it out of here alive!" He promised.

"What are you talking about?" The police chief blinked toward the door. Guilt and fear rose from his heart and now he was panicking. He wanted to warn his son away, but hoped he will run once the bombers begin their runs around 2AM as he heard down at the police station. He supposed to help evacuation, but he wanted to make this last run; this facility – he thought the government was working on something big in here....

The group leader stood in the middle of the room, around him, others stood around a stone. The group leader spoke in a language the chief never heard before. It wasn't even the distorted language of the Land of the Aggressors. His mind wondered far away, understood and resigned that he will not make it out of here alive. He could shoot them all, but it seemed that would have been pointless as they prepared to die anyways. Yet he was still lusting toward the truth: are these people actually worked for the Republic or for the Land of the Aggressors? What was their main goal to achieve here?

"Chief, you wanted to know, what are we doing here?" The group leader finally turned to him.

"Yes!" He was salivating, feeling so close to the truth.

"We've worked on a retro virus, but the virus already seen combat. Preliminary results suggesting it is the perfect solution: one hundred percent contagious and one hundred percent deadly!"

"You are killing us!" The chief was horrified.

"No, that is far from the truth! We are not even citizens of this planet!" The man looked proud and torn his sixth finger off of his hand.

The chief went pale.

He was mortified.

All around him the people torn off their sixth fingers, showing their true origins...

"Super soldiers?" He asked after a while as he couldn't think of anything else.

"No, chief! We weren't even born on this planet! We worked in deep cover, hiding in your society. What goes out there with Akron and your enemy; goes big time in the galaxy! Now, learn our past and our future, as we burn!"

The group leader invited him to the object in the middle and as the chief spotted the mysterious object the first flames and with it the heat arrived from the basement.

Young Erin was scared in the dark. Occasionally bombers flew past where his father left him, dropping their deadly payload into the city, but the resistance kicked in: fighter jets flew over him, shooting toward the beach head where the enemy tried to land more troops.

His father was the police chief of the city, a mighty position and his father took him most of the time to all those great places; arrested smugglers of all kind, but he was really obsessed with the building he entered not long ago. He used to tell him that it was a secret government lab, where they were messing with human genes to make super soldiers! It sounded like a great fantasy and so he begged him to accompany him...

Suddenly the earth shook under his feet. He grabbed a pole, and turned around. Way past the growing mushroom cloud an even bigger mushroom cloud emerged, than another one! He knew it was bad, the government and even his parents were saying that it was a last resort, if all other means of winning the war failed.

All of a sudden he became nervous. He moved closer to the metal door and touched the handle. He screamed in pain: it was so hot to the touch, it burned his palm!

He took a peek thru the high window and spotted a hand. He took a step away to see better and realized it was his fathers! His hair was on fire, the skin burned off of his hand as he shouted something! He just couldn't hear it. He stood there petrified, watching his father burned inside, alive, while showing another arm. When he spotted the arm, the burning fingers, he ran away

Chapter Two

Suddenly he was awake. Although the room was shrouded in darkness, he could see the shade of a young girl standing beside his bed.

"Here you go Papa, a glass of water for you!"

"Thanks Zoe!" The man sat up in the bed and wiped off the sweat off of his head then drank from the glass.

"Papa, don't worry about the bad dreams, they'll pass!"

"Yes Ma'am!" Erin gently smiled toward her and went back to sleep.

By the time Erin woke up in the morning, Zoe left for school. She left breakfast for him.

He thanked his late wife for the little angel in his life.

After the war he got married, entered to the service. They were rebuilding Akron, day by day. Zoe was just a baby when one day he came home and the neighbors were all inside his apartment. They were crying; they literally attacked him upon entering into his own home. It took him awhile to grasp the seriousness of the situation: his love of life; his wife was dead, stepped on an IED on her way home from the market!

Assassins from the Land of the Aggressors, he was told.

He took time off and his life went downhill. Little Zoe spent more and more time with grandma while Erin became fat and ugly. He was drinking, smoking and taking pills too.

One day, in a clear moment he grabbed his hand gun, loaded it and pushed against his temple.

He remembered like it was yesterday: sunny day, early spring. He turned toward the window, said his good byes and he was about to pull the trigger when he heard a cry of a baby. His mother never came to pick her up! In that moment, there, he felt guilty. He felt his wife was looking down to him from heaven and he felt her lips pressing on his face, uttering: "Don't let me down, take care of our child!"

He went to rehab, cleared his system. He returned to the service and took up his responsibility as a parent, albeit sometimes a strange one. He raised her to the best of his ability, but somehow he felt their relationship was strained day by day. She believed all the nonsense about the end of the world, the drained natural resources. He thought this was perhaps just another phase in the young adolescent girl's life, but as months passed he realized, he might has to live with this for a long, long time.

He figured he might take her to a ride along when school goes on the late spring break in a couple of weeks. Just how his father used to do it with him…

He thought this would be a great idea as he chewed his breakfast; gulping a good tea with it.

"My little angel will be a good wife of somebody!" He surveyed the remnants of the breakfast than realized if she will move out of his house, he'll have to find a woman who could take care of him. That made him sad. His track record for dating was close to zero since his wife passed away, but he knew, he needed a companionship.

Zoe always told him he looks handsome, but he wasn't sure it is because he is her father or because he was a handsome man after all…

His beeper went off; the office called him for a new case. By the time his car arrived with his aide he was shaved, dressed and ready to work. He picked up a half empty case of cigars and left the apartment.

"How are we doing today, sir?" The Corporal had asked.

"Mr. Tok, I was born ready for this job, you better learn to be here before they call me for a new case!"

"Yes Sir!" Tok saluted and allowed the Chief to take the driver's seat.

"Do we know anything?" Erin asked his assigned aide.

"Only that the owner of the building was contacted after one family of the now dead person couldn't get in touch with their relatives!"

"So is this will be a suicide case?" Erin frowned.

"Mass suicide, there are seven dead bodies, littered around the apartment..."

"What?!" Erin swiftly turned toward Tok while driving.

"Sir!" The Corporal pointed toward the intersection. Erin hit the break hard and the huge car stopped; marking the dry asphalt with tire marks.

"I hope they closed down the crime scene!"

"I could call the police station to inquire!" Tok was quick and by the time he finished the sentence he was calling in, thru the car's built in phone. This was a new technology. Erin had this wired into the police cruiser two years ago, when the second relay satellite was launched into orbit. While Erin called the bulky device the channel of the devil, he acknowledged that the private, scrambled line was way better then calling thru the security forces radio channel...

Chapter Three

The case & the girl

Erin pulled to the curbside and exited the vehicle. He flipped his badge at the police woman at the entrance to the four story high, grey, nondescript house. The victim's apartment was on the fourth floor. It was bigger than the other rents, but warmer during the summer and colder in the winter.

He walked thru the entrance and spotted the first body, face down. It was a male in his mid-thirties. Another body laid on the floor two steps behind. Erin frowned: "Is the coroner on his way?"

"Yes sir, he is bringing another refrigeration truck with him. They should be here in about three hours..."

"Good. Call the photographer and get some fingerprints! Tell the others not to touch anything!" He walked deeper into the apartment, swarmed by cops. It didn't take him too long to see the pattern: the victims were running scared before they were gunned down. Erin suddenly stopped. There was a woman, face down on the kitchen floor.

"Curious..." He uttered and bent down. There was something that bothered him: no blood on the hard floor. He turned the victim; saw the horror on her face, eyes still open.

"But, chief..." Corporal Tok arrived.

"Where is the blood? Where is the entry point?" Erin glanced up. He was visibly troubled by the discovery.

"Sir, the photographer didn't finish. They have not moved the bodies yet, but checked for pulses and weapons, but found nothing."

Erin touched the woman's body, and found no entry point. He turned her around and checked her back.

"Huh!" He moved closer to her and sniffed into her blonde hair.

Tok kneeled down: "What is it sir?"

"It smells burned!" Erin frowned and moved the victim's hair away.

Soon they both stared at a black, smoldering hole.

"What is that?" Tok was the first to speak.

"Damn if I know, but this isn't made by a regular bullet!" Erin stood up. The entry point was way clean. He walked toward the entrance and then bent down to the first victim. He carefully checked his body and found a similar wound on the guy's chest.

Tok swiftly followed him.

"Check the others!" Erin ordered him with urgency in his voice.

Tok returned shortly. He uttered into the chief's ears: "They all look like this!"

"That's a problem! Call for backup, absolutely no press! Tell the morgue guys that I'll be at the autopsy and keep this development quiet! Find the owner, I need to talk to him, find out who were these guys, where did they work! I need to contact their employers!"

"I'm on it!" Tok nodded and left.

Erin walked out to the street. He needed some fresh air and he wanted to smoke a cigar badly. He found the cigar box and pulled out one really great blend. He began to chew on it, then as the taste hit his brain he went for the lighter only to find out he forgot it!

He looked around somewhat desperate and saw two reporters lurking around with a camera. Not the kind of people he wanted to ask for anything. He turned around and spotted two tall women talking halfway down the street. Both were blondes, both were tall and skinny, good looking too as far as he could tell.

As faith would have it he approached the left one: "Excuse me!"

The woman with blonde curly hair turned around and she flashed her perfect smile.

Erin was taken aback by her natural beauty.

The world stopped spinning for a moment; all his problems, his past, the loss of his parents, his angel, Zoe was all forgotten; as if like his life distilled and all that remained mattered: the woman, her smile and her beauty…

"Can I help you?" She asked with a strange accent and the most sensual voice he ever heard.

"Do you have a light?" Erin almost begged. She was more than beautiful; gorgeous and perfect! Her blue eyes radiated warmth and genuine interest. She frowned lightly and checked her pocket. As smile crossed her face, she pulled out a small oval shaped object. Erin had never seen anything like it, since the Republic had strict guidelines regarding to any firework, including lighters that had to be square shaped.

She hit the top and the light erupted from the other side.

Erin shyly moved his cigar over the light and it lit up. As he moved closer he smelled the scent of her perfume and for a moment he felt dizzy. He never smelled anything like it; she was truly exotic. He saw the map the other blonde was holding, so he asked: "Are you ladies lost? Can I help you?"

"As a matter of fact we are! I'm here to visit my father the first time in many years and we need to find this address" She showed him a piece of paper.

He nodded, he was happy he could help them in return: "Not far from here! Three city block to the west, one street up, at the intersection turn right. The house will be on the right side around the middle of the block!"

"Thank you for your help, mr…" She trailed off playfully.

"Erin, Chief Erin!" He flashed his smile, hoping it would mask his two days beard. Suddenly he thought he should've had his neat leather coat.

"Mr. Erin, it was nice to meet you, my name is Aa and this is my girlfriend, Miss Haas!" The exotic woman replied with warm smile, she was certainly interested in him.

"Maybe we'll cross paths one day again!" Erin trailed off. Actually he was hoping with all his fibers it would happen soon, but unfortunately there was nothing else to say…

"I would like to think so!" She kept her smile while the other woman grabbed her arm and pushed her down the street.

Erin took no shame to watch them until they turned at the corner. He loved her smile, her cheek bones, her eyes and the whole package. He rolled back his memories, playing it over and over and he felt some pleasure when he realized he did use the proper ethics, introducing himself, not mentioning his full, married name, hereby granting the idea of being single. He smiled as he remembered: she would use only her given name as well; she probably was single too!

"Sir, The owner is waiting for us!" Tok suddenly arrived.
Erin was still daydreaming.

"Sir?"

"Oh, yes Tok, let's go!" He agreed reluctantly and tried to remember to the scent of her perfume. It was slowly slipping away and he just wanted to bask in the memories as long as he could...

The owner was in genuine shock and seemed confused. He said the four guys who rented the place were quiet ones, never late with a payment, never drunk and never in trouble.

Yet as Erin pointed out they were all dead...

The search went well; they all had IDs on them. The police collected the evidences and took them back to the police headquarters so they can run the names in the database.

Erin didn't like the situation and his day just tanked when Tok came back with the coroner in trail.

"Sir, the four male victims worked for the City Preservation and Archeologist department."

"What?"

"Do you want me to repeat it sir?" Tok paused for a moment.

"No! Let's go to their building. What did they say? Is the director still there?"

"He'll wait until five PM!"

"Let's go then!" Erin glanced at his watch. Time was the essence... He smiled briefly after realizing how this statement contradicts the job titles of the now deceased, then pointed ahead.

"What about the autopsy?" Tok reminded him.

"I'll be there after I talked with the director!" Erin gestured dismissively and then realized he should call home to see if Zoe was all right.

Zoe spent the day in school like most kids in her age. In class they joked about her 'husband', her Papa but today were Wednesday and she agreed to tutor one of the girls from math. The equations were getting too difficult for most of her classmates, but not to her. She daydreamed most of the day anyway -she could look at any one of the exercises and tell the final outcome or outcomes if the answer had a possibility to be a negative or a positive number without using a paper and pen. The teacher left her alone after last week's embarrassing lecture when Zoe had to point out that the teacher in fact was wrong. All hell ensured, the director was called in, but he knew she was smart, he let her explain her view on the subject and by the end of the day she showed not just the whole class, but the faculty as well that she was right, the teacher was wrong. The answer spoke to itself on the board, unquestionable and the class was enthusiastic. Zoe knew they hadn't had the slightest clue about the exercise. It was an extra hard one, meant for the top five students of her class. They were lost too. Zoe had to admit, she wasn't even bothered herself with that one, she was studying integrals and her mind slipped to the more juicy subject. She wanted to write prime number calculating software for their home computer her father bought last year. That was her latest, monthly project.

She arrived home around three o'clock in the afternoon and after whipping together something to eat later for herself and her Papa, she greeted her girlfriend and they sat down in the living room with the math books.

Greeta was street smart, but not really smart when it came to science. Zoe considered her to be a good friend; somehow they clicked together. Perhaps because Greeta was growing up without a father - her mother and she had to do everything around the house including cleaning, fixing things that broke and cooking. They even traded recipes occasionally for cooking exotic food.

Greeta just left when the magical device; the house phone rang. Zoe knew well, beside her teachers practically nobody had a phone in their houses. It wasn't just the price tag that was attached to such a priority device, but the years long waiting times discouraged the most hardcore fans as well. She heard from her teachers that sometimes others come to use the phone than leave small gifts around. However his papa wasn't the most social person, no wonder nobody bothered them...

"Papa?" She picked up the receiver.

"Darling, I've got a new case and it's a difficult one! I'll be home late! Are you going to be okay?"

"Yes Papa! I'll leave the salad in the fridge for you! There is some bread left as well! I'll get more tomorrow, just leave couple more coins on the table!"

"All right darling, be safe and sweet dreams!" Her father hung up.

Zoe stood there for a moment. His voice was strange. He was serious about his job, as always, but something else was in the air. It took her awhile to realize he sounded happy and preoccupied even for those short minutes when he called. She wondered why, while she fell asleep - alone in the house.

Corporal Tok pulled up to the front entrance of the City Preservation and Archeologist Department just couple minutes after five. Erin took little time to admire the huge sign on the meticulously clean front lawn and walked straight in. He flashed his ID card and marched beyond the security guards.

"Where to?" Erin barked toward Tok, who pointed to one of the elevators. Erin disliked the mechanical devices, even though the police building had two for personnel and another one for ammo.

Erin wasted no time to walk thru the main hall.

The receptionist stood up, watched them pass by then sat down to reach the internal phone line to warn her boss.

"Can I get you a drink perhaps?" The heavy set man offered a wide smile in the otherwise huge room. Erin walked thru the thick, leather padded doors; Tok walked after him and quietly closed them.

"Administrator…?" Erin wondered off as he realized he forgot to ask Tok about this guy's name.

"Oh, my name is Jasuf Nhal, at your service! Would you like some tea perhaps?" The administrator added, pointing toward the desk and the small cups hoping that they would take off after and he could go home, but knew from countless meetings that the best and fastest way to end the conversation is to try to give them something to run after…

"Mr. Nhal I believe you're aware of the situation. Seven workers of the City Preservation and Archeologist department are dead, killed by an unknown assailant. I need to know everything about them. What were they working on, who they were? Their files and yearly reviews along with any notes your physiological department might have."

"Yes, I thought you might need their files so I already instructed my secretary to talk to the Human Resources department. They will compile their files for you; the department will copy everything we have on them. It will be ready for pickup by tomorrow evening!"

"That is a fast response, administrator!" Erin said barely masking his surprise. He expected more bullshit from a man who practically ran half of the parliament.

"I know this is a horrible event and believe me, I don't need the media attention on this. After all midterm elections will kick off in about a month!"

"Oh, how could I've forgot!" Erin smiled. No wonder...

"Would there be anything else chief?" Jasuf Nhal asked politely.

"Can you tell me what project were they working on?" Erin accepted the herbal tea, as it was customary from a polite visitor.

Nhal frowned, he forgot to check it. He walked behind his enormous, wooden desk and browsed thru his papers.

"Well..." He said and lifted the phone. He called the secretary who had even less luck to figure it out.

"If you would just wait for one second!" Jasuf himself was curious now and he took time to turn on his personal terminal. The screen slowly came back to life, but the codes flashing across his screen reminded him it usually takes an exact bathroom break to get to the prompt. He had no idea whether the IT department can speed up the boot up process nor did he care. He found the waiting time awkward however as he had no way to escape to the bathroom without leaving his guests alone.

"Ah, finally!" He let out a satisfied smile and went for the keyboard. He found the myriad letters awful distracting on the keyboard as he usually leaves this sort of work to his secretary, but after a couple minutes he found the right directory and brought the files to the screen.

However another obstacle presented itself in the form of a warning: 'Access Denied' sign.

"Is there a problem administrator?" Erin took a hesitant step toward the desk.

"Uh, please Chief, just sit down!" He pointed toward a chair while he called his secretary again to ask for the password. He was lost and he hated the feeling. It meant he wasn't in control. The very idea horrified him as so many people depended on his competent decisions every single day...

He was tired and exhausted by the day's work, after all he was the administrator, and as such high in the food chain must have a lot of work... besides daydreaming...

The secretary told him the password, he typed it in and the files opened.

"Well, Mr. Erin, it seems they all worked together on a classified mission!"

Erin frowned. He didn't expect that. What kind of mission could be classified for an archeological team?

"They were carefully excavating the area at the now overgrown B sector..."

"Is that on the edge of the Northern Hills?" Erin tried to remember why it left a bad taste in his mouth...

"That's correct. The area is still un-cleaned. Lots of wreckages from enemy fighters and overgrown trees along with weeds make the dig a treacherous one! Not to mention of the possibilities of unexploded ordnances!"

"Well, did they found anything? Maybe they found a special ammunition cage or the second rumored nuclear bomb the Land of the Aggressors had…"

"No they never had another bomb! Trust me, I would know!" The administrator replied with a snappy voice.

"But the news was even on Aas's radio show couple years ago!" Erin protested.

"Aas is a bright man, his show is pretty good, but he was wrong on that one!" Nhal acknowledged the famed radio host's show, than read into the file. "Actually they were sent there as far as I can tell," he tried to read the small letters that made up the numerous sentences "because recently we began to reconstruct the blueprints of the city how it existed before the war and we found some discrepancies. There are more buildings then permits were given and this area was rumored to have an office building that belonged to the government itself. We want to find out if this claim was true so we sent this team to excavate in the area and search for any clues if our government was involved or not!"

"Do you have an address for me?" Erin went pale, his legs went numb. He almost had a panic attack as the administrator said the address was: "5452 N. Maximillan Ave."

"Chief?" Nhal sensed something was wrong, but the chief practically jumped up while he offered his hand. "Thank you for your time Administrator! My aide will be here tomorrow afternoon for the files!"

Jasuf Nhal accepted the hand and watched the two men leave his office. What a strange fellow -he concluded.

Erin didn't speak until they got to the police cruiser. Once inside, Tok turned to the chief. "To the dig?"

"Okay!" Erin nodded. His mind was somewhere else. The past was creeping up and he sure didn't like it one bit.

It took them a good thirty minutes to get to the address. Erin gazed toward the roof of the unearthed building where tree branches were moved aside forming a big pile. He was here before once; standing near toward the entrance, waiting for his father to return almost twenty years ago...

"Are we going to look around?" Tok brought him back to reality. The sun was setting toward northwest, turning the sky into red and orange. Carnage, he remembered back to that particular night... He touched his left palm where the burn marks were still visible and said: "Tok call the station and ask for a steak out team for the night and leave a message for the morning shift to close this down as soon as the sun comes up!"

"Why not now?" Tok inquired.

"If this place is really what it supposed to be..." He trailed off. Sure it was. It had to be... Probably their own government was behind it and they were watching now. *Wretched killers*!

"Sir?"

"Tok, drop me off at the station. I'll go to the coroner; you'll go and relay my orders personally, not thru the radio!"

"Why?"

"I have my reasons! Go!" Erin dismissed him annoyed by his aide's persistent questions...

By the time he got home it was late at night. He stopped at the corner store to buy some bread and farm milk for the morning; than before he took a cold shower he left some coins on the table for her daughter for the morning.

He hoped the cold shower will take his mind away from the past, but of course he was wrong. He had a miserable night and he was up around the same time as Zoe was.

They made breakfast together and as they sat down she giggled. "So who is she?"

"What?" Erin didn't realize he was actually smiling. Again...

"The woman!"

"What woman?"

"Papa, you are day dreaming. This hasn't happened with you in a long time!"

"Well..." He burst into a smile.

"Do I know her?"

"No, she is a visitor to this city! I think." He added after recollecting one of his most precious recent memories.

"You think? You better ask her out!" Zoe giggled.

"Naw, I don't even know her address." He shook his head.

"How did you meet her?" Zoe felt excited. Her Papa finally met somebody!

Erin told her as much as he could say about the case and about his desire to light a cigar and he forgot the light...

"I always thought smoking is bad for you, but maybe I am wrong on this one!" Zoe laughed picking up every subtle clue.

"I told you, I don't even know her address!" Erin shook his head.

"Of course you do! Didn't you tell her how to get to her father's apartment? Papa you've got photonic memory!"

"Uh, a woman as pretty as she is probably has a husband or boyfriend!" He shook his head sadly.

"Did you see a ring on her finger or did she say her given name?"

"No, but..."

"You said she was with her girlfriend, right?"

"Yes."

"That means she has no boyfriend otherwise she would have to introduce him to his father."

"Now you say something..." Erin actually never thought of that.

"All you have to do is get a dozen of white Cimber tonight, go to her father's address and you shall be in business!" Zoe gave the marching orders.

Erin smiled on his daughter, then changed subject. "How is school?"

"I didn't embarrass anyone this week!" She shunted her eyes.

"Yet!" His father slipped his tongue. "I'm proud of you, I was never good in school, that's why my father started to take me with him along the way; to show me what if I go down like those criminals, but I tell you what, when early spring break comes, you can tag along with me once or twice, okay?"

"Oh, you are so sweet, Papa!" She went to hug him.

"You make me so proud! Your Mama would be so happy. She was a lab scientist for a medical corporation; she would want you to be a scientist to follow her carrier!"

"Ah, then a humble man would take me away on his white electrical car, yeah?" She teased him. He used to say that to her whenever she pissed him off.

"That's right!" He stood up just as the doorbell rang.

"It must be Corporal Tok! I got this, Papa!" She pointed to the dirty dishes in the sink.

"Be good!" Her father kissed her forehead and left.

Erin watched from his car as the police erected the white extreme-caution tapes around the block. People on the street walked by slowly and stopped to see what the commotion was all about. He gazed toward their direction and spotted two blonde women. Just like the other day. He frowned. No, they can't be here; this is far away from downtown...

But the left one had curly blond hair, just like his mystery woman the other day. He jumped out from the car and charged toward the middle of the crowd. He lost eye contact with the women's hair and when he exited from the crowd the other side; he didn't see any of them...

"I must be daydreaming!" He thought then turned around and headed toward the entrance.

"We've found some notes and a case full of tapes here!" Corporal Tok showed the Chief the backpacks. The names on them were a match.

"Pack'em up, but take fingerprints first. Maybe we'll find something on them!" He nodded and walked past the officers. He smelled the wet dirt; the yellow mass towered on both sides. He couldn't believe how quick the vegetation overran this place.

"See, Chief, they only got till' the door" Tok pointed toward the thick, black door.

Erin abruptly stopped. There was the same door he touched almost twenty years ago. He wanted to be alone.... Or just run away...

"Did the police men found anything suspicious on the roof?"

"Far as I know, the archeologists didn't dig from up there!"

"Well, then Tok, how did they knew to dig here, to reach the entrance?"

"Good question sir, but we found holes on the other three sides too. Maybe they got lucky…"

"Or maybe one of them knew this place before. Let's find out from the city archives what other buildings stood here during the war and perhaps businesses too…"

"You think..?"

"I don't think anything; but let's just be thorough with this one!" Erin sent him away.

Chapter Four

His late night visit at the coroner's office left him speechless. Just like in those sci-fi stories when the dark green mutants came from space to slaughter the innocents, the coroner assured him that the only reason the victims died shortly, because something burned thru their bodies and left a hole in each and every one of them. Most disturbing was his personal theory about the shooter while he speculated about the precise shoots. Most of the victims were shoot right at the heart, but two of them got the hole between their eyes.

"Very disturbing" The coroner said who was a retired Navy Seal. He used to kill precisely in that manner, just with bullets. Erin went back to the archeologist's apartment to check the floor. There were some burn marks where the bodies lay, just as the coroner said it would. His theory revolved around some very precise plasma burns, but he had to do further research on the bodies.

Of course Erin had to caution himself; as he might be going wrong on this all together. Maybe the dig had nothing to do with the victim's deaths, but before he would make the hasty conclusions he had to wait for his aide to return with the victim's files from the City Preservation and Archeological Department.

Erin slowly inched toward the door of his worst nightmare. He never told anyone about his father's true death. He told his mother it was a blast that killed him. Of course his remains were never found...

He inspected the door. He even banged on it. He listened to the sound. It was like a sea sailing ship's door; seemed thick and bulky and it was barely rusted! He would've thought after twenty years in the ground it would be in worse condition. Then next to the handle the recent remains of a wielding caught his eye.

He frowned. He gently touched the piece as if it would still be hot to the touch and inspected the door's new seal. It was relatively fresh, still gleaming at couple of the spots. It told him that somebody was inside not long ago; perhaps less than a week. That was strange... -he thought. He grabbed another cigar and slowly walked up to the top. He could see the city's skyline almost intact from where he stood. Then he remembered that the apartment of the victims were on the other side of the city, beyond the skyline. He radioed for Tok.

The Corporal showed up with a cold drink and a sandwich. He took the food and told him to check up on the victims. See if any one of them had a car.

"Why?"

"We found no car at their apartment, but call the owner and find out if he knew anything, then call in for the girls" he implied on the secretaries in the police station "to check the Motor Vehicle records."

"Why is it so important?"

"Because the question looms; how did they get home from here? If they owned no car and it's a possibility, they would take public transportation. Somebody might saw them, noticed something. If they took a cab then we can inquire further. Maybe they were followed, maybe..."

"I understand sir!"

"No you don't!" He shook his head. He didn't want to tell him his theory that the archeologists were inside. That they might found something, something so interesting they all went home to investigate further, where they were killed...

He found the other police officer who was in charge of setting up the cordon. He told him to get some samples of the roof material and send it to a lab for analysis.

He watched as the forensic team arrived, took samples of the wielding and they took one sample of the edge of the door. Their diamond cutter broke right after that making the team leader very angry.

Erin glanced up to the hot sun and gestured to Tok: "Let's go and pay a visit to the coroner!"

The man wasn't happy. He showed microscopic samples that made Erin no sense and spoke about the highly precise weapon the assailant must have used.

"What is it mean? Can you tell me plainly?" Erin lost his patience after a short while.

"All I can tell you that this isn't a plasma weapon. I consulted with my buddies in the military and I came to the conclusion that this is the work of a laser gun. It has to be. No other explanation exists! No microwave experimental weapon is this stable and or precise, but a laser gun would be. The only problem beside the fact that it isn't exist that even if it would, the generator would be so big, it would need so much power, it would have to be nuclear!"

"What?!"

"Case closed, it has to be nuclear and even if it is it would have to be a huge one. I heard the military has been experimenting mobile power plants that use nuclear fuel from old weapons and they are allegedly cooperating with the Aeronautics and Space Agency of the Republic (ASAR) for future military satellites. I think they would be low powered long term power stations, so you would need couple of them together. So you see the guy might hold the weapon itself, but the power cables would go down the stairs, out to the streets where couple trucks would have to be standing!"

"You should be a sci-fi writer!" Erick shook his head.

"You think so?" He brightened up, hearing such encouragement.

"Seriously, this will not fly with my boss and frankly, not even with me!"

"Consider this: It was a precise shot! They knew where the vital organs were, and if not, a shoot thru the brain always works. One shot per person, no goofing off, man they were experts! No visible sign of strangling, but I did found strange chemicals in two of the victim's bloodstreams. I had to send it to the lab for further testing. It's not alcohol and it's not a poison, so far I know that much. I took samples of the burned skin and there are no residues of anything metal or any chemicals. What can I say, it was a clean shot!"

"Soon the forensics will bring some metals in for testing, send it to the lab too!" Erin left with more questions than answers.

He had to meet his superior for a status update and he had a hard time figuring out what to say...

Chapter Five

"Chief, how are you doing? Have a seat!" Police Commissioner Rally Adams was eager to hear from his top Chief. He needed to inform the mayor of Akron later on regarding to the seven victims.

"Thank you sir!" Erin took up the offer; beside, he had no choice either.

"So tell me, how is the investigation going? Is there any good news I would want to hear?"

Erin imagined a stop button on his life right now, but then he would never meet the blonde again. At that moment he decided to get some flowers and meet the girl tonight. If he survives the grilling, that is.

"Sir, I don't think you have to worry about follow up mass killings…"

"Oh, based on what?"

"On my own gut feeling!" Erin responded quietly and as serenely as possible.

"I need something more! Something tangible!" Adams was swaying his head.

"Sir, this is a serious, specialized case. Whoever killed the archeologists, knew he can't leave any witnesses around! I don't know what the motive or motives were, but I might know more by tomorrow. What disturbs me the most isn't that they killed seven civilian, but the method they killed them. We have to keep that under wraps as long as we can!"

"I heard that it was some kind of experimental plasma weapon?" Adams moved closer and lowered his voice.

"The coroner don't think so, he believes it was a laser gun of sort."

"Are we watching too much sci-fi lately, huh? Next thing we know, the dark green robots are invading the city of Akron! Get to the bottom of this Chief, get to the bottom of it fast!"

"Yes sir!" Erin was busy nodding.

He was hoping corporal Tok picked up the files from the City Preservation and Archeologist Department as he walked beside the cubicles where the other cops were working. He inquired by his corner desk he rarely visited, whether his assistant returned or not. As it turned out he was on his way back, so for next thing he called his house. His daughter promptly picked up the phone.

"Papa, how are things going today?" She just finished with her homework and was hoping to make some punch pudding with seeds in them. Cooking was somewhat interesting for her, because sometimes things without any reason were good, sometimes so horrible it had to be thrown away. She also heard the boys might like a girl who knows how to cook and she definitely didn't want to miss that train...

"Sweetheart I'll be in late, so late that you should go to sleep and don't worry about leaving anything for me, I'll be okay!"

"Make sure you buy her some flowers before showing up at her father's house!" She giggled then disconnected the line.

Erin frowned, like he needs a secretary at home too...

His desk phone rang, the receptionist reported that corporal Tok arrived.

He waited for him to bring up the files and jumped on the first one.

"Hi boss, I talked to the house owner of the victims, he said they had no cars, something about the allowances of their pay grade didn't allow it."

"It's all right let's assume they had none. Have somebody talk to the bus company see if they picked up any larger groups from that area that would fit the descriptions and call the cab companies too!"

"Yes sir!" Tok went to his desk and started making phone calls.

Erin checked their files. Five of the archeologists were interns; two of them were actual employees. One of them rented the apartment for the interns and for himself, the other one lived with his wife, who made the initial call. He made a mental call to match if the two employees were the ones whom were shot between the eye or not. As he scribbled it to a notepad his phone rang.

"This is police chief Erin, who is this?"

"You're not so happy buddy; the coroner!" The man replied on the other end.

"I assume you found something?"

"Nothing good for you I believe, come down when you have a chance!"

"I'm on my way!" Erin slammed the phone and was looking for his aide.

He caught him between two phone calls and told him that he'll take the cruiser tonight and left.

On the hallway to the basement he found about five police officers waiting at the elevator.

One of them turned to the Chief: "Hey boss I heard you are chasing deep green mutants from outer space!"

"I see you waiting for the inevitable Harl, the elevator that never comes!" Erin responded with mild sarcasm in his voice.

He took the steps to the basement and entered into the brightly lit room. He liked it, perhaps because the coroner wanted it to be bright and so he was exempt from the nightly shutdown procedure that affected even the hallways.

Some idiotic bureaucrat figured it would be a nice and fair game if the police districts electricity usage would be publicly monitored and measured against the fireman's.

He rolled his eyes for a good minute the first time he heard it...

The coroner sat by his sandwich on the table.

"Is it okay?" Erin approached him. The coroner's two assistant was gone already, they were alone in the morgue.

"Yeah, nobody else is alive to take my sandwich away!" He smiled, misunderstanding him entirely.

Erin frowned: "What have you find for me?"

"Nothing good I am afraid and I am afraid that maybe we don't even supposed to know about this case all together!" He cleaned his fingers with a napkin and walked to his workbench. "Take a peak!" He showed Erin the microscope.

Erin cautiously looked into the holes and saw some complex three dimensional set of balls in gray background.

"Interesting!" He concluded, not knowing what it was.

"No, it is frightening!" The coroner corrected him.

"Okay, what do we see in here?"

"Well this is what I found inside the two head case. You know, we're carbon based life forms, so anything non carbon based could be highly toxic for us, it can't dissolve. The live picture you saw was the first if its kind I ever seen; it is silicon based! Most likely some form of truth serum if the layout would roughly the same if we would see a carbon based equivalent of!"

"I presume it doesn't exist?" Erin grimaced while massaging his forehead. He apparently developed a mild headache from this case.

"Correct and while we are at it, let me tell you what else doesn't exist!" He dropped the plastic bag on the desk. Erin recognized the piece from the entrance door he ordered to be cut. The coroner grabbed the bag and wiggled it front of Erin before put it down:

"See its okay, I am not a metallurgist, I know composite materials exist, we use them all the time, it makes the actual product better, but this baby has thirty two metallic composite, and seven of them doesn't exist in our periodic table!"

"Not good?" Erin peeked up, toward the coroner, who shook his head.

"Now about you're wielding… That is usual. Industry grade material, used by professionals only!"

"Thanks, finally something ordinary!" Erin seemed relieved. He fiddled with the evidence for a minute. "So what do you think, how long until some shadowy government official shows up and take over?"

"Could be any moment" The coroner shrugged as he checked his watch. Erin thought the same, than he remembered of something: "By the way, you're a married man, right?"

"Yes…" The coroner frowned.

"Where can I pick up a perfect dozen of white Cimber around this time?"

Erin was lucky, the coroner knew a place, although he seemed skeptical regarding to Erin's intentions. At the force they looked him as a loner... He drove in the night and parked the car, occupying almost two regular car's length. He snorted on the small electric cars, plugged into the curbside meters. He didn't need that one and he smiled as he passed them after stepping out of his car. They wanted to give him an egg box too, about a decade ago, but he refused. He protested; he became a pain on the ass for anyone, just to get noticed. He wanted a gasoline fueled car and no batteries beside the one that held the power until the next time he turns the ignition key.

Chapter Six

He turned his attention to the flowers beside him. "I've made it this far!" He made a face, feeling paralyzed all of the sudden. He felt scared just like the first time he kissed a girl in the school's backyard. He frowned upon recollecting the old memory and grabbed the flowers: "I have nothing to be afraid of!" Snorted and slammed the cruiser's door hard. With strong steps he was at the door of the apartment building in no time. He walked thru the door and went straight for the fourth floor, stopped front of the second door on the right and knocked hard, before he would change his mind and run away.

He tried to listen quietly, to hear what was going on the other side, but as he inched forward the door opened and he faced himself with the tallest man he ever met face to face. He was at least a foot higher, biceps strong as a gun; the clothes seemed tiny and tight over his muscles. His forearm was full of tattoos; he was bald and wore dark sunglasses.

Erin swallowed hard. He didn't expect that...

"Can I help you?" The man asked with a strange accent.

Erin let out a shy smile: it was the same accent the blonde woman, what's her name? 'Aa' had.

"I am here to ask your daughter out!" Erin forced the air out of his lungs.

The bald man frowned.

"I presume, your daughter name is Aa?" Erin continued shyly.

The frown deepened. "You may presume it! Hold on just for a minute!" He held up his index finger and closed the door.

Erin wondered if coming here was such a great idea at all. He might end up in a body bag…

He heard some commotion from the inside, then the door opened wide and the bald man attempted to smile. "Please come on in and forgive me for my sparsely decorated living room!"

Erin walked in and looked around the practically empty room. Beside an old mirror, there was a table and couple of chairs, the worn wooden floor and the big emptiness. 'Sparsely' was a huge understatement!

He noted three persons standing around, looking all nervous, like they were being made.

"The man in the corner is Josh Kulighan, my half-brother and that is Baby Haas with him, ah, here is my daughter!" He smiled toward the opening door at the other side.

Erin's eyes were glowing as he spotted the slender woman. She had some blue, almost skintight pants on – later he learned they were called jeans, and abundantly available where she was from -and a tight T-shirt. She blushed when she spotted him holding the white flowers.

She moistened her arched lips and said: "Hi Erin, I remember you!"

He shook by the deep and sensual voice and then quietly offered the flowers.

"Oh they're beautiful!" She took it and took her time to adore the flower cup's design, like she never seen it before.

"Well, khm, I was wondering if you might consider going out with me, perhaps as soon as tonight!" Erin was sure the father will cut him in two and send him back to his own daughter for a cookie material…

The girl seemed distracted for a moment; she even frowned and turned toward her father's half-brother, then glanced toward her father.

"I know this is unusual, but... I can't get you out of my mind!" Erin smiled to cover his uneasiness.

"Uhm, let me change into something better and we can go, please give me five minutes!" She disappeared along with her girlfriend.

Erin knew this will be the most awkward moment of the night; to be left alone with the no doubt angry father and his half-brother...

Mr. Kulighan as Erin remembered disappeared thru the dark hallway to the kitchen and returned shortly with a plate full of small cups and a bottle of clear drink.

"Would you try something special, only of course if drinking alcohol isn't a problem for you?" The man asked.

"Well normally I don't drink, but at one time I was considered a pretty heavy drinker!" Erin decided to try something new. Not like he didn't drink anything alcoholic since he found himself again, but avoided it largely to teach his daughter to some good manners.

"This is quite strong!" Mr. Kulighan warned him as he mixed the clear drink with something reddish.

Erin cautiously moved toward the cup. It seemed extremely small and sniffed into the air as he picked it up. It had a strong and exotic smell, just like the entire evening. He shrugged, than gulped up the content at once. He felt his lungs were on fire at instant! "What the hell was this?" He tried hard to clear his burning throat.

"I warned you about its strength!" The man rubbed his fingers together in an apologetic manner.

"But I didn't know, whoa, this is still burning! What's it called?"

"Charblin with vodka." The father stepped closer and added. "Forgive me my manners, I haven't even introduced myself, my name is Diesel!"

"It's all right, as your daughter said my name is Erin, just plain Erin!" He forced himself to say 'plain' to help them understand his marital status, but it seemed they don't care or understand, because they kept continuing to apologize about the strong drink. It was interesting that they had no tea, but he guessed that alcohol was their tea...

"You can eat something dry to absorb the alcohol if driving is going to be a problem!" Mr. Kulighan tried to be helpful.

"I'll be careful, but I doubt it, after all I'm a police officer!" He tried to brush off their concern.

"Is that so?" Diesel seemed interested all of a sudden.

"Yes, sir! Police Chief Erin, actually!" Erin felt slightly dizzy. That alcohol was strong indeed!

"Well, then my daughter in good hands! Excuse me!" He bobbed his head toward Erin and left the room to find his daughter.

Aa was putting some mild make up on with Baby's help. When she saw Diesel walking in, her face darkened. "I know the drill, you told me already! Be cold, be annoying and get him lost!"

"Actually I want you to be the opposite! Turns out he is the police Chief. He could be useful for us in the near future! Befriend him and try to find out why the police shut down the remains of the lab!"

"Yes sir!" Aa saluted and walked out like a cat.

Erin's yaw dropped when he spotted the fox. She had a two piece black dress on, with matching high heels!

"I'm ready, let's go!" She smiled at him and all of Erin's problems evaporated...

"Nice, big car" Aa said as Erin pulled off the curb.

He tried to assert his options. Beside the point that he was hungry he wanted to offer other options as well, among them to sit in the park, but it was late already.

"I'm glad you like it!" He acknowledged her compliment. Indeed the cruiser was in top notch condition, with no scratch on the side, the extra layer of midnight black paint was almost glowing in the night just like he was...

"So if you are a chief, is that mean you're an investigator?" She asked while steering thru the window, out into Akron's nightlife.

"Yes."

"Are you working on anything right now?" She tried to downplay the significance of the question, by smiling at him, hoping he would take it as an encouragement.

"Of course, the city pays me only for work! I don't have time to relax too much, you know I have goals!" Erin completely fell for the ploy.

"It's nice to have goals, I have those too. Only that I have to set the bars very high, so I don't reach them too early!" She replied somewhat amused and like a good politician, never revealing anything concrete about her.

"Oh?" Erin didn't expect that as her answer. She was different from the women he met before. They would never say that. He remembered to ask her about dining in the city, since she never inquired where they were heading: "Are you hungry?"

"I am starving!" She smiled.

"I can tell, you are very skinny, not like it is a bad thing!" He added quickly while slapping his imaginary self with something hard. 'How stupid can I be?'

She turned to him, her eyes glowing. She wanted to scare him, tell him that it is only an advantage if one is on the run if one is to be the hunter and not the other way around, but calmed herself and said only: "I spent most of my life south, near the Demilitarized Zone. Not much food there!" She heard that on the radio the other day, after her group learned about Agross V's horrible past.

"I've never been there, actually I haven't left this city most of my time." Now Erin had to clarify himself, not to seem too hostile toward the southerners... "No, I mean I went to the beach, of course I did, I went to visit the farmlands too, but I never ventured that far south!" He said.

"It's not much to live for down there!" She smiled, turned her head to see the intersection ahead. He was actually cute, she concluded. She remembered Smith; the man who changed her life about seven Earth years ago and she shuddered for a moment. She wondered what he will say once he lands on this planet in about three weeks from now. What will he say to her? Officially and other wise... Will her quest with this alien man will make him angry or he will give her his blessing? She and the others were on this planet because of a life and death matter, but their job, their objective to retrieve the item had failed so far. It supposed to be an 'easy' mission, since this was a humanoid culture as well, except perhaps the fact that these people had six fingers on each hand instead of five. She looked down on her hands, touched the prosthetic finger, which was attached surgically to her; small price to pay. Sure as hell she never imagined this life when she was running for her life in Delta City's dark alleys, killing for money to buy food, get high and party… Smith pulled her out, showed her the way, showed the light, offered thrilling possibilities of who she was, so she would be proud of her parents she never knew. She thanked her newfound life to him and in a way she had a crush on him ever since. So she had to be careful for many reasons, but she knew Smith probably would never choose to be with her, for many reasons and she wasn't getting any younger either. If she had a chance to grab a man, even for a short time, she would go for it.

Erin on the other hand was nervous. Will she run away once they begin to talk and he has to reveal his daughter's existence? He contemplated the idea of telling her up front, before even getting into the car, but now it was too late. He was hoping that the restaurant owner remembers him and allow dine in the reservation only establishment. He did some favors to the owner of the Delicatesse of Akron before and it was time collect the deed. He parked on the left side of the road; taking up about three spaces reserved for handicapped electrical vehicles only and helped his date out of the car.

People were sitting by the outside tables, drinking, laughing; the servers were running from table to table, it was a busy night for the restaurant.

Aa frowned for a moment, after two guys pointed toward her and said something that she couldn't decipher. The language of Agross V was fairly easy for her, to speak, but even though she understood most of it, some made no sense to her what so ever.

Erin was looking for a familiar face, and once he found the waitress he knew, he walked up to her. "Dear Almana, do you remember me?"

"Chief, how can I forget your help!" The woman in her late forties smiled warmly.

"I wondered if you would have a small table for me and my companionship... Maybe I can talk to Laz, see if he can hook me up?"

"No need for that Chief, bring your beautiful companionship with you, there are always some VIP booths in the back, but I am sure Laz will pay a visit himself!" She showed them the way inside.

"This is nice!" Aa peeked over the booth's divider to see the open tables. The dimmed lights made her feel cozy ; stark difference of her usual position on her space sailing warship's brightly lit bridge...

"And the food is excellent!" Erin promised, although he hasn't been here over a year.

Aa heard a small cough from the isle and spotted a well-dressed, immensely tall, skinny man, with a bottle in his hands.

"Laz?" Erin greeted him and offered his hand to the newcomer.

The man in question accepted it and showed his gift: "Please accept this fine sparkling wine from the restaurant, enjoy your stay and if you need anything special, just let Laz know, I'll take care of everything!" He assured them.

"You seem to know all the right people!" Aa concluded aloud while smiling coyly.

"It seems that way isn't it?" He cracked up. He was on the right track. "Have you decided what you want to eat?"

"I was hoping you could recommend something for me!" Aa replied. She was in trouble over most of the items on the menus, not knowing what the exotic names would really mean.

"I'll get you something really good!" Erin nodded and a waitress seemingly appeared out of thin air, bringing two glass of water and took their orders.

The exemplary attention of the waitress displayed didn't go unnoticed for Aa, who inquired. "How come they all over us like that?"

"I helped to take care a small problem for Laz, to clear his son's name... and the waitress outside was just a really nice person the last time I brought my girl here..."

Aa paused for a moment, giving him a blank stare while Erin turned red. "Oh, I mean my daughter, the only one!"

"You have a daughter? Are you a single father? What happened to Mrs. Erin?" Aa seemed shocked for a moment than she asked all the questions without thinking.

"I'm a single parent. Her mother passed away long, long time ago..." Erin seemed to be withdrawn as he told her that.

"I'm sorry, I didn't mean..." Aa recognized her mistake, and touched his hand for solidarity.

"It's all right, you didn't know..." He shook his head. He was sad Aa could tell, but at the same time, he seemed to be grateful for her physical and emotional touch. She saw he needed some encouragement: "So what's your daughter's name?"

"Zoe, she is an angel!" He replied immediately, brightening up.

"How old is she?"

"Twelve, but sometimes she seems older, you know. I tried to raise her to the best of my knowledge but recently she changed and I don't know how to be close to her again... Is that makes any sense to you?"

"It does, she is probably looking for friends..."

"She doesn't have many, I think she is too smart and her classmates ridicule her for that. Let me tell you, last week the principal himself called me as she managed to embarrass the entire faculty!"

"With what?" Aa's curiosity emerged again.

"Oh, it was about some high level mathematical problem. As much as I understood at the end she was right and the teachers were wrong... I was never a good student, so I really has to rely to my daughter on that, but embarrassing the teachers aren't a good way to lead I think!"

Aa giggled. "I must meet your little angel, I already like her!"

"Really?" Erin seemed shocked. *This woman was definitely different...*

"Of course, she reminds me a little bit to my childhood, although I never really had one either. I mostly grew up with my uncle. I never knew my mom and my father stayed out of my life so long...."

"Is she died in the war?" Erin tried to be tactful while gaining insight into her mind..

"Something like that..." Aa eluded any specifics, herself not knowing the whole truth... Let him think it was their twenty years old civil war, than some intergalactic mystery – she thought.

It was Diesel who opened the door as Aa walked up on the stairs. Kulighan told her how exiting their evening became when they tested the surveillance equipment and everything worked out of the box; a first... While they expected no trouble, they had to be careful not to 'excite' the local population.

"It seems this went well!" Diesel stated as he looked over the woman. Aa was thrilled and ecstatic: "You have no idea!"

Truth to be told Erin was somewhat shy or perhaps the customs were different, either way it was Aa who had to make the first move for the good bye kiss in the car. She could tell Erin was interested in her... He watched her entering into the building, then left.

"Can you give us a report now?" Josh walked up to her impatiently.

"About every little detail?" Aa giggled.

Josh stopped dead on his track, she was something...

Aa disappeared into her room to change back into something more comfortable. When she emerged she had a story to tell. Partially she was excited she managed to get some information out of Erin, partially she was excited because he was such a handsome man...

"All right guys, this is screwed up, but I think he is looking into our lab issue. The reason for the continued police activity is because the excavation team or some members of it are in trouble."

"What kind of trouble?" Josh frowned.

"I don't know yet, but I managed to memorize two names that were on top of the pile in his car's back seat."

"Well, no wireless signal in the city, so we concluded they're just not that advanced." Josh stated.

"I'm sure you or Diesel can find a way in if there is a network of any kind!" Aa shrugged. She learned different methods of network penetrations over the past few years, but had little experience on alien systems...

"That will be on us tomorrow to learn it!" Josh bobbed his head. "When are you two scheduled to meet again?"

"The day after tomorrow, it is the sixth and the last day of the week. He is off and he asked if I would like to go to his house, meet his daughter and they supposed to cook for me!"

"Going to his house already?" Baby bumped into the conversation, smiling.

"You know me, if I wanted that way, we would already been in his house!" Aa casually shrugged and left to take a shower.

"Tough little cookie!" Diesel concluded. Actually he enjoyed working with her as she was pretty professional, even when she was relaxing. The girl was a perfect agent. No wonder Smith yanked her to be on his team. Then again Smith was a man too and no matter how pleasing Azure has been, he knew Smith partially kept his eyes on Aa over the years. Not just as a co-worker, but as a personal friend as well... Then again it was really not his business how friendly they got with each other, as he had his own master and the older Emperor was unforgiving enough to warrant his compartmentalized mode of thinking about Smith and the others. Then again... He always found Smith and Aa's platonic relationship so romantic... He was no longer a literature teacher, but if he would've remained on the path he would definitely find some time to write a novel about the love between the immortal Smith and the mortal Aa.

"I agree, she is tough!" Josh frowned after Aa and walked away to think about how to get information on the two names she wrote down on a piece of paper.

Chapter Seven

Zoe just woke up. She heard a humming noise from the kitchen: it was his father, singing!

She put up her morning clothes that were resting on her chair from the night before and walked quietly to investigate further.

As his father turned around he spotted his daughter, smiling at him.

"What's up sweetness?"

"So when will I meet her?"

"Who?" His father pretended to play stupid.

"The mystery woman!"

"Why are you saying that?"

"Papa, you are humming! The radio is off, and you always listen to PS (Paranoia Station) morning show!"

"Okay, okay, she is great, you know, like how grownups kind of great!" He added, frowning at her daughter who busted out laughing.

"It's all right!" She patted his hands and sat down on her usual chair. His Papa had made breakfast already; he probably was up early...

"Do you have something nice to wear? I invited here for lunch tomorrow, so we have to figure out what to make!"

"Oh, I'll take care of that!" Zoe nodded seriously. She hasn't seen his papa so happy in a long time, she was so proud of him!

Erin left to work; he spent most of his day in the police station where he sat behind his desk and read the files. He tried to find something, anything that would point him toward the right direction, but these were simple people. Tok reported that the MV records came back negative; none of them had a registered car. His aide pointed out that they could have stolen one, but Erin knew; these were honest people. Tok also reported about the inquiry: he asked some questions from the wife of the other lead archeologist, but learned nothing unusual.

"The Commissioner is on our case, I need some new leads!" Erin turned to Tok.

His aide grimaced, like there was nothing to say.

"Tell our men to double their effort. Call every cab company and send officers to the bus depot to conduct a full blown investigation!"

"I am on it!" Tok nodded and left to take care of the business.

Erin scratched his head: he needed witnesses... Nobody heard anything in the apartment building, nobody seen any thugs, people snooping around, but of course if the government's special agents took care of the victims, then they would've left nothing useful behind... He was about to leave for the day when his desk phone rang: Commissioner Adams asked him to join him...

"How is your investigation going?" The Commissioner was blunt. He asked as soon as Erin closed the door.

"Not good boss. No witnesses, no leads! But I tell you if it wasn't brown aliens and it was indeed our own government then maybe the Interior Ministry should tell us to stop this costly investigation!"

"On the other hand if I do inquire and they say no, they might come in and take over, have you considered that?"

"I did!" Erin nodded.

"…but have you considered what they might do to us whom might learned something interesting about the case?" Adams moved closer and turned his voice down.

"I see your point!" Erin nodded realizing the reply's true meaning.

"So tell me you have all available men making inquiries and doing the best they can to find a witness…" The Commissioner lay back on his seat.

"That is correct! By early next week I should have something"

"You better, and tell me about this alleged building they worked on! Is that still so interesting for us that we have to blow money and resources on surveillance?

"If the archeologist found something, whoever killed them might return." Erin pointed it out.

"How about lowering our profile? Have a patrol car there at night and frequent passing during the day, that way more officers available for the quest!" Adams offered some changes.

"I tell 'em to wrap up the mobile police station by Monday morning!"

"Make sure!" Adams lifted his index finger, before letting him out of his office.

By the time Erin arrived home it was pretty late. Zoe was waiting around after she finished most of her homework. As her papa arrived she jumped from her seat and ran to the front door.

"Hello sweetness!"

"Hi papa! Let me show you the dress I selected for tomorrow!" She forcibly pulled him into her room.

He checked out the deep blue blouse, the long skirt, frowned and turned to her. "That isn't you!"

"But I want no trouble!"

"No trouble at all! I know my little daughter. She would never wear these skirts, maybe a one peace dress…"

"I have a grey one!" She lit up and searched her wardrobe. While she selected the new dress, her father looked around. "What's wrong papa?"

"She'll think you had no childhood. You know I don't even understand the titles of at least half of your books. You're sure you want to be a professor?"

"Professor? I don't want to be that!" Zoe frowned. Her papa had strange ideas.

"What do you want to be then?" It occurred to him, that he hasn't asked that question in a long time…

"I want to be a scientist, I want to go to space, and I want to do great discoveries!"

"Oh, darling can't you be somebody more useful, like a doctor?" Erin had no idea about her new fantasies.

"Papa, I can be so useful to my country as a scientist! We, the Republic have to be in space so if the Land of Aggressors ever rise again, we could escape and live…"

"They never rise again, I don't think too many of them left alive!" Erin disagreed.

"I promise I won't bring it up in the conversation myself!" She put her left hand over her chest.

"Have you figured out what are we going to cook for our guest tomorrow?" Zoe asked.

"I have some ideas…" Erin smiled.

Chapter Eight

Baby walked up on Aa who surveyed her weak dress collection. She contemplated the idea of just wearing jeans and polo, but as a first invitation for a lunch it seemed formal enough to warrant something more exotic.

"So is that guy really handsome?" Baby asked as she sat down into the chair in the corner.

"You have no idea!" Aa blushed.

"You like him, do you?"

"Sort of… Don't know if it is because it's short term or not, you know. On the Executor I'm the Captain. Nobody dares to come up to me like that and I am proud to be the Captain!"

"Smith made you a Captain. You're now a respected member of the space forces, what not to like in that? You report directly to the Admiral himself. Do you ever miss your old life?"

"Sometimes, but I probably would be dead by now. Smith showed the way, I owe my life to him!" Aa became emotional serious.

"He always shows the way, that's why he is our leader!" Baby nodded in agreement.

"Tell me, you never had a chance to be with him? You knew him when he was just a teenager…" Aa wanted to ask that for a long time now.

"Of course there was a time for that too, but we agreed that if I'll be the leader of the Imperial Honor Guard I can't occupy his personal life!"

"Huge price to pay…" Aa mumbled.

"Yes. Would you give up your post to be with him?" It was Baby's turn to inquire.

"Hard choice, but perhaps I would. Do you think it's true what he said?"

"What's that?" Baby frowned.

"About that alternate future where Tri'ng died and he married me, we lived happy, or at least until I died...?" Aa bit her lips.

"Toxic confirmed it, I mean a Starship that came from the far future and can talk, feel and be alive... Organic spaceship... If that can be a reality in one day, I guess you could be Mrs. Smith...."

"I feel a tad guilty going out with Erin. I feel I let Smith down, I wonder how angry will he be when he finds it out?" Aa wondered.

"You have feelings for Smith. Don't think for a moment he has nothing for you, but whatever his intentions were, he has to honor the code. Azure saved his life and she didn't have to. That is something very powerful. He knows that and tries to repay her kindness. We know she is a fifth generation pleasure model converted solider from the far past, in reality she is less than two years old not seventeen! It is truly amazing. I mean I was in prison along with Smith; my mind was suppressed by the telepaths just like his, but I mean I thank the Emperors for her every day, to even consider freeing our leader, Smith!" Baby concluded.

"You know," Aa pondered, "I feel ashamed. He put me into the right position before he was arrested and deported along with you and the others. I feel guilty; it should've been me who organized the rescue. I mean all I should've done is to talk to the Admiral and call Josh Kulighan. He had firepower under him too..."

"Well, if you would've rescued us, he would be obligated by the code to follow your personal wishes; maybe you two would be together..." Baby winked.

"Yeah, that may be..." She smiled with a sour face, and then added: "Even if I can't be with him, at least I have to do great things, so I would live up to his expectations!"

"That is a very tall order!" Baby shook her head, disagreeing with her statement.

"You've seen him, I mean the things he can do, tell me about it!" Aa demanded, although she saw him in action too, she saw how he could impose his will on others if he wished to...

"I was once with him on the planet Gnem..."

"The first planet he bought..." Aa nodded.

"He gave a speech...it was before the palace was built downtown. I mean those people are poor, most had no money for transportation, so they walked. It felt very powerful and I could sense his discomfort. He didn't want to be their leader, but as far as I could see, until the horizon I saw nothing but people. There were millions of souls in every street corner, on every rooftop in every balcony and they all listened. They kneeled down when it was time for a national prayer and I tell you that if he would've said that come on, follow me, we have to kill our enemies they would've followed him from the age of toddler to the age of a retired citizen. That was a very powerful moment in my life. I understood a lot!"

"That's why he is the Emperor!" Aa just realized.

"So what are you going to wear for your date?" Baby Haas asked, while smiling.

"I have the right dress in my mind!" Aa smiled and showed her the light, beige, summer dress.

"Child, he'll be all over you once seeing this!" Baby couldn't stop grinning.

Chapter Nine

Erin could barely concentrate on driving. The woman, who sat beside made him feel to be extremely lucky. She wore a one piece dress, like it was sawn by hand. Small holes allowed his eyes to wonder under it, seeing her perfect curves; he wanted Zoe to be gone! When he realized that, he felt ashamed, he has to show good manners, lead a good example for her daughter.

"Man it will be hard!" He mumbled.

"What will be?" Aa inquired innocently.

"Oh, solving my case." He tried to jump subjects and think of something entirely different than the hot babe beside him. "You know there aren't any witnesses, but my men are working on it around the clock." Erin tried to push his dirty thoughts far away by exposing his work. After all she was a visitor, she knows nothing of his past, his city's past. 'Not yet' a little voice inside his head told him.

"So those diggers are still missing?" Aa implied they were nothing more than cheap labor, hopefully to make Erin explain his case in finer detail.

"They aren't utility workers, you know, they worked for the City Preservation and Archeological Department!" Erin read Aa's expression and noted, she didn't understand him: "See for some time now the National Museum trying to draw a complete two dimensional picture of the city and among other things a 3D mold, miniature replica as well, for the War Museum. So a lot of buildings have been destroyed at the end of the war, when the Land of the Aggressors unleashed their nuclear warhead on the Republic and we tried with conventional weapons to respond, but they were attacking the city from the south by land, and from the northern plains by bombers and they had a beached too. I remember as the bombers flew past me and my father, dropping their deadly loads on the besieged city. Then the leaders of the Republic decided to fight back with a nuclear warhead and at the end we had more. They capitulated three days later, but it was a madness, whole sections of the city disappeared by raging fire..."

"What were you doing with your father outside? I mean you should've been with your mother in the shelters!" Aa asked, then tried to cover her emotional laden angry outburst.

"Well, since we became friends, I guess I can tell you that my father was also a police chief. I told you I used to be a bad student a bad kid in general, so my father took me along with him to arrest people, to do detective work, so I would see where that dark path takes me if I don't become a good student. I was with my father, who supposed to help with the evacuations, but he got what he always wanted; search warrant for an address and it was Sector B, 5452 N. Maximillan Ave!" Erin tried to read Aa's face, but the woman sat calm on the seat.

"The same address those archeologists tried to excavate..." He added.

"Oh, then it's personal!" Aa realized.

"More than that! I lost my father that night, but he firmly believed government agents used that building for cover up work of some kind, maybe to create a super soldier!"

"What made him so sure of that?" Aa was all ears now. Every bit of information could help her; after all she knew that this mission is extremely important for Smith.

"He used to tell me that he saw people in there that had only five fingers!" Erin opened his eyes wide, signifying the claim. Of course that isn't how that happened, but nobody has to know that...

"Five fingers! How strange!" Aa tried to hide her excitement. This confirmed they were in the right place!

"Well, don't tell your father or any one, but those archeologists are no longer alive..."

"Suicide?" Aa tried to pretend to be dumb...

"Homicide and I have a gut feeling that they found something and somebody killed them for that! The only thing I don't understand that if our government is behind it why haven't they stopped me by now or why have they killed them at all. Well I said too much, I hope that this information will stay between us and not see the media!" Erin felt guilty all of a sudden. It wasn't like him; he used to be good with work secrets...

"I swear my life to that!" Aa turned to him, touched his hand and she looked death serious.

Erin was taken back for a moment. A minute ago he was confident, his slip was a mistake, now she looked like she would stand beside him in a stand up and could trust her with deadly confidence.

"Nice house, nice neighborhood." Aa surveyed the street. Erin lived in a three story apartment building in an upscale part of the city.

"Zoe is very excited!" Erin added as he showed her the way.

Zoe sat by the door in the past half hour and listened to the noises. Sometimes she climbed on top of the chair to peek out of the small, decorative top windows.

As soon as she heard his papa's voice, she jumped off the chair, took it back to her room and opened the door before his father could insert the key.

She couldn't take off her eyes of the tall, skinny woman who shyly walked thru the door. She carried herself with a certain kind of confidence, and her clothes were made for her! She just stood there speechless, looking the beautiful blonde, her skintight dress...

"Zoe, this is Aa." Erin cleared his throat, to raise attention.

"Are, are you an angel?" She finally managed to ask something.

"Why would you say that?" She bent forward, to face straight into her eyes.

Erin's head turned slightly to the left. She had a wonderful body. He managed to shake the sinful thought out of his mind as Zoe replied: "You are so beautiful, you know how to dress and I love your red lipstick!"

Aa slowly smiled upon hearing the appraise: "I only heard good things about you!"

"Really?" Zoe blushed. "I should check on the food, we may need to heat it up!" She ran away embarassed.

"I'll get everything!" Erin jumped right in the middle. He had to walk away or may just kiss her right now... She was insanely hot in the dress and the leather underwear made his dirty mind wonder and salivate for more...

"So this is your room, huh?" Aa walked into Zoe's domain. She saw lots of books in shelves from walls to walls. She tried to find some toys but spotted only two stuffed animals and some posters about a boy band. Obviously she either tried to mask her child hood life or she was just really a book worm type. Something about her however heightened her senses. She could never be a mind reader, telepathic like Smith, but because of her father she could feel people's intentions if she concentrated hard enough...

"Yeah, there is my bed in the corner and my dresser, the school books and some other books, then in the left side, that big box on the floor is the computer; on top of it is the color printer! Papa bought it last year. This is so advanced it even has a monitor!"

"Where are your toys?" Aa finally asked what she thought was missing from the room.

"I don't have many; I never had time for them." Zoe shrugged, than added: "I had to learn how to cook long time ago after all I was growing up with my father, who learned alongside me. Then I always had to do some cleaning, washing and it takes the time away. Not like I miss it, I mean there are great mathematical and physics book around me, they are so exciting, you know!" Zoe shrugged again, partially to downplay the significance of the missing toys, partially to strengthen herself.

"My heart goes out for you, I never had a childhood because I lost my mother around the time I was born, my father moved out and I stayed with my uncle but from my experience I can tell you to just enjoy playing! Play as long as you can!" She kneeled down to the floor and touched her cheek.

Zoe was taken back. She frowned. *This woman was strange.*

"Be careful, not to rip your dress!" She pointed out.

"I can get another one if I want," she waved in the air dismissively "but I heard you are a smart one. I can tell by the way you look, the way your room is decorated. You may have an exciting life ahead of you. I would only wish that my brother would be here!"

"Why?"

"I would ask him to do a telling on you for me!"

"Your brother is fortune teller?" Zoe frowned. *Strange brother…*

Aa smiled, but her smile was a sour one. She just realized; she will never measure up to Smith… "He is more than that, but the tellings are special!"

"Why is that?"

"They all come true, all the time!" She said in a fashion that Zoe's back shivered from it.

"So if he is a magician, what would you consider yourself?"

Aa wanted to say that she was a warrior, but had to remind herself about her undercover assignment. Smith wanted them to stay low, not to reveal these people that there are aliens around them… "Well, little angel I would consider myself a more material girl, who believes in science, but in a way he is a scientist too…" She referred to his 'brother'."

"How could be a scientist a magician? That is contradictory!" Zoe disagreed.

"All right, let me show you an example!" Aa walked up to the desk and lifted a battery powered light. She turned on and checked. It worked. She smiled and theatrically placed into her open palm and asked: "So how does it work?"

"The light?" Zoe frowned: "Easy. The tube holds three batteries. When I push the button, the circuit closes and electricity flows thru, therefore the light bulb comes on. Why?"

"So you told me in a scientific way. What would you say to someone say about two hundred years ago, before the discovery of the electricity. Could you explain to that person in three sentences in a way that he or she would understand it?"

Zoe bobbed her head. "Man, that's some powerful thought there!"

"Well, my brother can light a wax candle without a match, and there is an exercise where the candle being in a glass bulb. I tell you it looks like magic when he makes it light up!"

"That's not possible!" Zoe shook her head, firmly believing she was right.

"Well, as a bookworm I can see how it might be impossible for you, but believe me, the universe is full of magic!" Aa touched her face.

Zoe felt her hand; she had a smooth touch. Her fingers were manicured and painted bright white at the end. Suddenly she wanted that too...

"There are beautiful pictures I got on my disk Papa picked up at year's end with the computer about stars and solar systems nearby! They were taken by the best telescopes of the Republic! I would think there is no magic out there, but science!"

"True, but in a way science is magic. Once you realize that you are the children of the stars and the stars are the children of you, you are from them and they are from you! One day you go out there among the stars and may meet someone not look like you. There will be some excellent chances to share this revelation with them. They will appreciate that thought!" Aa spoke from her heart.

"Do you think there are others out there? I mean in space?" Zoe felt Aa was a very special person, for some reason she not just embraced but believed what she said. That was a rarity among her friends...

"There is nobody out there, but the food is ready!" Erin popped in his head, smiling at them.

Aa was playing with one of the stuffed animals. She turned her head back and while she smiled, she looked directly into Zoe's eyes: "I am certain of it!"

Zoe chuckled. There was something how Aa replied that made her hair stand up in the back of her neck.

"All right ladies, let's eat!" Erin tried to change the subject, he was certain it was pointless.

The food was delicious; Aa really liked it and inquired first at covertly, then in the open regarding of which one of them did that particular dish. Erin had a great time seeing her daughter getting along with Aa so easily. It filled his hearth with warmth. Aa even ate from the desserts he was sure she wouldn't. It was late in the afternoon when they finished talking about the past, about family stories. Aa was an avid listener. She revealed less in return, since she had to hide a lot more of her troubled past than them, but overall they had a great time.

Erin was quiet on their way back, but before he got out opening the door for her, he kissed her. She passionately returned it. "When will we meet again?" She asked with unusually deep voice.

"How about Tuesday, I have to work, but maybe we could meet and we can pick up Zoe from school? Usually I pick her up on Tuesdays. It's a bonding kind of thing!" He apologized.

"No need to explain it, honey!" She replied as she kissed him again.

Chapter Ten

"Well, you two seemed cozy enough!" Josh stated when Aa walked thru the door.

Diesel looked her from top to bottom.

"What?"

"You are looking unusually petite!" He voiced his observation.

"Do you have a problem with it?" Aa asked defiantly.

"No, but I would think it's a waste. You would be better paired up with a fellow warrior!"

"Like you?" Aa lifted her eyebrows. Diesel never expressed any interest in her...

"No. My life is set, I must follow my master, but whenever I work with Smith and his crew I feel I have more freedom!"

"It's a weakness, sir!" Josh cracked a smile.

Diesel thought about it. "True, but it feels good even to indulge my sensors, my brain with someone so gorgeous like Aa, who isn't just attractive, but deadly as well. No wonder Smith had an interest in you!"

"Yeah, hot and deadly ladies, like Baby!" Josh added.

"...But there is a difference," Diesel added "While Baby is a professional, Aa is family." He referred to Smith's past, how Aa's father trained him to be a killer.

"As soon as I change, I'll fill you all in how it went!" Aa left for the other room.

"Well this is disturbing, but logical!" Josh summarized it in one sentence after they all listened to Aa's tales.

"What is?" She asked innocently.

"An AOCP (Alliance of Central Planets) cell, hunting for evidence, to get rid of all what remains, but it could also mean if your Chief is right, that maybe they didn't found it yet! You need to find out more about the archeologists. I would love to take a closer look at the dig, but unfortunately we won't measure up to close scrutiny, so I will not risk it until they completely gone."

"We may have to go to the spot where they were killed. It shouldn't be hard; considering we now know where they worked and have two of their names. It should be easier to gain access to that information from a civilian department then the police..." Diesel concluded.

"That may be, but the best we can do right now is to contact Commander Rick onboard our floating base, the SCC (Space-Craft Carrier) to contact the Admiral. He has to find any spacecraft the AOCP might have around orbit!"

"What if they landed here and used their cloaking?"

"Well, it isn't really my concern, but if Smith wants to keep this society's development undisturbed, we might have to find it! We have to keep it under surveillance and prepare for containment..." Josh thought it out loud.

"First we have to find the damn spacecraft, which I doubt we will from here as our friends have more chance to do it from orbit, although these paranoids here make that hard too!" Diesel pitched in.

"I'll send Baby to the meeting point tonight! Diesel you'll drive her to the beach, so she can make a sight to sight contact with Commander Rick and communicate our findings and intentions to him!" Josh finished the briefing.

"I am hungry!" Diesel touched his stomach.

"I guess its precooked rations or the local foods again..." Josh scratched his head. He was hungry too, and Aa was done eating for the day...

Chapter Eleven

Erin sat in the car and barely listened to the radio. Aas, the host of PS (Paranoia Station) was talking about secret agents flooding the city, but nobody knows who they were and what there is objective...

His mind was on Aa. He was dreaming of her; kissing and touching her. He wanted her bad that was not a question. She was an amazing woman, but sometimes strange. She could speak with so much passion and so much certainty he would follow her to the end of the planet if there was such a thing...

The car leapt over an intersection and the shocks kicked in, hereby bringing Erin back to reality. They were on their way to Northern Lights, a cab company where a dispatcher sworn to Tok, one of his drivers picked up a group of seven or eight persons in a minivan type of cab... Erin tried to concentrate what he had to say, what to ask, but his mind kept wondering under Aa's tight dress.

"His name is Mr. Alok, he has been with the company for seven years. He is a dependable guy with a wife and two young kids. He was one of my best drivers..." The dispatcher said, away from his desk where chaos and madness walked hand in hand. He said he could go away from his desk for couple minutes before he loses track of his work. Erin already lost it...

"So if he is so dependable, where is he?" Erin looked around. He was standing in the first floor of an old factory building. Countless of technicians were working on broken cabs, mostly beneath them.

"My guy disappeared the day after he picked up eight persons from the address your aide asked me in sector B. He came in the morning, picked up the cab, but came back later, said he doesn't feel good and needs to take off for the rest of the day. He seemed tired and unfocused, so I let him go. That was the last time I saw him."

"Do you have a picture and an address for us?" Erin asked.

"Sure thing, I already made copies!" He said giving him a thin packet of papers.

Erin glanced at the driver's large scale picture. He nodded: "We'll let you go back to work. If he calls or anything…"

"I'll give a call to you, yes!" The dispatcher nodded, already half way back to his booth.

"I guess, we are going to the address?" Tok asked.

"Correct, call in to the precinct and request a stake out car for that address!"

"Okay boss!" Tok sounded excited as he opened the police cruiser's back door for him.

Mr. Alok's wife was a huge woman in every direction. Erin was taken back when she appeared in the doorway. She was surprisingly nice however. She was worried about his husband who came home early from work and said he was afraid. He left out the next morning and he was gone since, but dropped off a note saying he thinks he is being followed and he has to hide.

"Does he have any relatives?" Erin asked the obvious while looking around the neat living room. Everything pointed to the direction of a stable, loving life. Mr. Alok seemingly went nuts, but Erin suspected something more. He believed in the missing cabbie, his nightmares and that somebody follows him...

"He has a sister living in the countryside. His parents passed away last year." Mrs. Alok wept quietly.

"Do you have a phone?" Erin asked.

"No, no we don't have one. Why?"

"I need you to contact my number as soon as you hear from him. It's very important. I can help him, but I need to know more about his fears!"

"What did my poor husband did? You think he is being followed?"

"We don't accuse him of any wrong doing, but he is a person of interest in a case I am working on. He may be the only witness..." Erin trailed off.

"You must return him to me!" Mrs. Alok grabbed his hand.

"I try my best ma'am!" Erin said, ready to leave.

By the time he got into his car Tok confirmed the stake out car.

"We have to post a general missing person file on him immediately! I've got the sister's address; I'll contact the Rural Commission's office as soon as we return to the station!"

"You are serious about finding him, are you?" Tok took a peek in the rear mirror, to see his boss's reaction.

"You've seen what happened to the archeologists. He'll join them unless we find him first!" Erin was gloomy.

Two hours later the massive manhunt was on. He spoke with the Rural Commission's office and got granted for temporary jurisdiction in connection with his case, a necessary step to go far south, before one would reach the Southern Demilitarized Zone. He allowed the local cops to investigate the matter, question the sister but he wanted the results on his desk as soon as it was possible. He was hoping to catch the driver within a day and ask him hard questions if he had to. He was after cold blooded killers, nobody else had to die! He went upstairs to see his boss. He needed some paperwork to put the driver in protective custody and he didn't want to wait for it with the driver at his side. He wanted it to go as smooth as it could!

Adams seemed happy to do something. He was probably pressed day by day from the Mayor's office.
Erin went straight home. He asked Zoe about homework, she showed him and he nodded like he understood all of it. A mental note popped up in his head. He seriously had to talk to the teachers to find out if she respected school rules or not. He knew well enough of himself to know he would play around them if it would be him and after all Zoe was his daughter, some traits were passed to her too.

Chapter Twelve

Aa surveyed her wardrobe and decided to wear something comfortable this time. She picked her favorite jeans, a white T-shirt and decided to get into the shower. She wondered what new she'll find out today about the case or will she have time to find out more about Erin's feelings..?

She knew that the Admiral was contacted and he ordered a sweep around the planet, but found no evidence of cloaked spaceships what so ever. He swept the planet from high orbit, but so far it was inconclusive. The Admiral reasoned quite logically that if the spacecraft was submerged or hid inside the cavernous mountains, it was almost impossible to find it. This task will most likely fall on Smith she concluded and wished he would okay her short term relationship. As her affection toward Erin grew, she was growing more and nervous about it... She knew for a fact that although Evan Smith spoke about the strict rules of not having romantic relationships in the past, he had a weakness in that area after all Josh Kulighan was an ex agent himself who was sent to an alien planet for five years and fallen in love with a woman and their love produced a child. When Smith came prematurely to pick the agents up for his fight against the Klons, Josh begged for him to save them both. As far as she knew his son was in college on SWEi prime, headquarters of the UNHL (United Nations of Humanlike Life forms), which meant they were both saved since his wife served alongside him on his lead SCC. She subconsciously drew the parallel between Smith and the people around him trying to be like him. Azure, Smiths love was no different and even the organic spaceship, the

Toxic mingled in things she shouldn't in order to save a life or two...

She just got out of the shower when somebody knocked on the door. Aa asked Baby to check on it while she grabbed a bathrobe.

When she approached the door, she spotted the police officer. She frowned.

"Are you Miss Aa?" The officer inquired shyly.

"I am!" She stepped closer, smelling trouble.

"I have a message from police Chief Erin. He say he is extremely sorry, but unable to come by today as he is busy with his case, but will come by as soon as it is humanely possible!" His eyes seemed to be glued to her body.

Aa eyebrows kissed each other: "Do you know if he is able to pick up his daughter?"

"I don't know ma'am, but it is unlikely, he is on his m...mission." The officer didn't want to be accused of information leaking about the ongoing manhunt...

"Thank you, officer!" Aa replied diplomatically.

"No date for you, huh?" Baby concluded.

"I have to pick his daughter up!" Aa seemed concerned.

"Now, you are playing Mrs. Erin?"

"Did Diesel and Josh take the car?" Aa let Baby's question go unanswered.

"Yes..."

"Then I have to leave now!" Aa replied and ran back to the rear room, dressed up in less than five minutes and was out to the door before Baby could say a word like how quickly she became emotionally involved with this alien family...

*

Erin grabbed the front seat with his hand and wished he would sit at the front. Tok drove the car like it was a race. The light and the sirens were on. Tok floored the pedal and drove in the middle of the wide Avenue avoiding heavy traffic on the side. They were in pursuit with another police car and about one city block ahead of them a modified electric car zipped in traffic, driven reportedly by their missing driver; Mr. Alok!

*

Zoe wasn't in a hurry. Her Papa was usually late anyhow, so she held a casual conversation with Greeta by the corner across her school. She occasionally peeked out to the wide avenue to see whether or not his Papa arrived with the black car.

Greeta must have seen something she didn't like, because she turned to her impatiently: "You must go now!"

"Why?"

"I've got company, and they're usually nothing but trouble!" She pointed at the two, tall and rapidly approaching girls.

"Are you in trouble?" Zoe asked, measuring her and the approaching subjects with her eyes.

"Sometimes... My mom owes them some money and they are good with extortion!"

"You should change girlfriends... Tell your Mama to move to better place and quit drinking!" Zoe said what was on her mind.

"Easier said than done!" Greeta shook her head, crossed her arms: "You should seriously consider leaving!"

"We friends aren't we?" Zoe wasn't moving.

"Yeah, but they are going to whoop my ass. You don't need to get involved!" Greeta replied, but it was too late. The older girl towered above them by then.

"Do you have the money?" The left one asked.

"Mama doesn't have it yet!" Greeta shook her head.

The right one slapped her face hard.

Zoe turned pale. She thought maybe she could reason with them, but she had no money on her either, and realized they were heavy hitters.

"What are you looking at?" The left one turned her attention to Zoe.

"Nothing!" She surveyed the concrete floor, hard.

"Look at me when I talk to you!" She grabbed Zoe's jaw and made her look up.

"Release her and you will not be harmed!" A sensual, soft, but edgy voice said from behind Zoe.

The girl holding Zoe's jaw looked up and frowned before laughed: "Cutie pie, better walk away before I mark your face forever!"

"My offer still stands!" The sensual voice turned darker in tone. Zoe recognized as Aa's.

The girl in the right smiled, shook her head and her ponytail shook along with it. She grabbed a knife from her pocket: "You should've taken her advice and ran!"

Aa was waiting for the girl to make the move. She leaped forward, knife face high.

Her senses heightened and before any of the standing parties could realize Aa's palms, holding the knife from both sides, stopped it before reaching her. The pony tailed girl paused for a moment. She didn't expect that and that was her fall. Aa's left elbow hit her face hard, while twitching the knife, hereby occupying the girl's hands. As soon as her elbow hit the face, she gave her a hard right hook with her other hand. A loud pop signaled the jaw gave out, the girl landed on the ground; unconscious.

Aa turned to the other girl, who before she could realize what just happened was grabbed by the neck. She ordered her half human muscles to tighten the grip and lift the weak body off the ground.

The girl knew she was in trouble.

"Look at me bitch!" She heard the deadly cutie's voice.

She was gasping for air, but the grip was strong as a vice, couldn't even think straight.

"Touch my girl again and I kill you!" She sounded calm, no sweat on her forehead, the girl in the air realized.

"Do you understand?" Aa shook the body in the air while clenching her teeth. She had to do pushups to stay in shape for the future, she realized.

The girl in the air tried to nod, but she couldn't. Her vision was fading out; she felt darkness and cold around her.

"I mean it!" Aa said it cold, then practically threw her to the ground and spun around. Zoe and her girlfriend was speechless.

Aa's dark expressions evaporated and the next moment she smiled: "Let's have some ice cream!" She put her arms gently around them, walking away.

Zoe soon concluded the ice cream was terrific, but her hands were still shaking, so as Greeta's.

Her girlfriend turned to Aa: "What would've happened if she gets up from the ground and drew a knife like her girlfriend did?" She referred at the end of the scene.

"She was too weak for a couple minutes and she had to scoop her girlfriend up too!" Aa downplayed the possibility.

Zoe laughed, although she still felt nervous.

"But what if..?" Greeta pressed. She felt it was a tactical error for a swift woman like Zoe's friend to turn her back on the enemy, but something in the back of her mind said she had contingency plans for that too…

"I've would have done what I promised to her…" Aa shrugged, licking the ice cream. *It was delicious*!

"You had no weapon otherwise you would've used it!" She continued to disagree.

Aa blinked, then pulled Greeta aside: "I heard you're a tough little cookie, helping your mother alone. I would've guessed that by now you realized: taking one's life not necessary requires other than the use of your own body." She contemplated the idea to tell her how to kill by hand, to stop one's heart by a reverse pulse, but decided she was still innocent enough. She changed her mind and said instead: "I could have killed her eight different ways and crushing her neck with my feet is the last one on the list. It's so childish, you know!" She winked at Greeta coyly who just stood there, the cold, melted ice cream dripping onto her bare hand.

Aa went back to the stand to order another one for herself. It was truly great!

Zoe approached her girlfriend: "Are you okay?"

"She is so frightening, yet so cool!" Greeta gazed after her.

"When I grow up I'll help you to get a good, stable life, I promise!" Zoe meant it. She had no idea Aa could do that…

Erin arrived at the house late. He was upset. He couldn't catch the driver; he escaped on foot, but was slightly injured. He was sure they catch him soon. As he entered the house, he heard female giggles. He then realized he forgot to pick up her daughter and felt ashamed. He hastily threw his coat toward the rack and walked into Zoe's room. He stood there dumbfounded: The three girls; Zoe, her friend Greeta and Aa played cards and drank fruit juice. They obviously had a great time. It was Aa who noticed him first: "I figured I should pick them up, since you were busy."

"How did you know where to go?" Erin managed to speak.

"Zoe showed me some pictures the first time and I remembered the school's name!" She said. It was true, but she also researched the subject for future use…

"Clever girls!" Erin smiled. "Should I pick up some food or…"

"No need for that Papa! The food is in the oven and it's still hot, waiting only for you!" Zoe giggled.

Today was full of surprises. Erin shook his head awhile later, thinking about it while he set the tables for dinner.

"This food is delicious!" Erin acknowledged.

"Yeah, and Greeta, Aa all helped. We still managed to do better than you!" Zoe smiled.

"Hey!" His father disapproved her comment.

"This was so great, I'll try to cook it later, see if my father and his brother like it!" Aa added. The food was relatively easy to make and she was confident she could substitute the local delicacies with UNHL spices.

"Papa, you eat like you never ate before!" Zoe concluded.

"I am hungry, worked hard all day long; you know I am a hammer!" He smiled.

"Yes Papa and I'm the wildflower!"

"What?" Aa was lost out on the joke.

"Didn't you have any nickname in school?" Erin frowned.

Aa couldn't remember what was the last grade she was in school before dropping out... She managed to add: "Yeah, Black Angel."

"I can see the angel in you, but you aren't dark enough for that!" Erin joked about her light brown skin.

Although Aa considered herself white, she liked to keep her skin tanned most of the time...

"Oh, it's because I brought death to my enemies, so they all wanted to like me!" She smiled.

Erin blinked for a moment, looked at her daughter who stopped chewing and Greeta whose hand began to shake.

Erin busted out laughing.

Aa did too to ease the tension.

The girls did too to mask their horror...

When Greeta left with a cab which Erin paid, he turned to Aa: "I'm surprised in a good way that you helped me out here!"

"Oh, don't even mention it. I had a really good time with them!"

"I was wondering if I can make it up to you somehow. Maybe tomorrow?"

"Aren't you working?"

"They call me if they need me!" Erin offered a smile, then added: "Corporal Tok took the car, can I call a cab for you?"

"Sure thing, and for future reference, here is my father's number. You don't have to call for a messenger!" She blushed slightly.

"I thought it was a nice touch!" He smiled.

"It was…" She kissed him and he kissed her back.

Zoe very quietly walked to the kitchen to give a little space to the grownups.

Chapter Thirteen

The beach & the helicopter conspiracy

"I told you there is nothing to report, but he didn't get any closer, because he was visibly disappointed!" Aa repeated again at the morning table.

Josh shook his head disapprovingly.

"I know you need information, but if I tie him to the bed he won't believe me!" Aa defended herself.

"Unless if it's for seduction!" Baby winked at Aa, distracting her for a moment.

"All right, try to learn something. I have no clue what to report home!" Josh was disappointed.

"What's the plan for today?" Aa asked.

"While you and your love boy hang out, we are going to the northern tip to pick up some equipment and food supplies from the SCC."

"During the day?" Aa frowned.

"Yes. Just this time. You know we don't want to establish any pattern, so I thought I throw some randomness in it!"

"So that's why you go in plain sight, huh? Not too smart!" Aa concluded.

"Just worry about the love boy!" Josh grimaced. He wasn't even sure the item they came to this planet still exists, but of course they had to stay at least until Smith arrived sometimes next week -he hoped. In the meantime he tried to penetrate the police network along with the City Preservation and Archeological departments.

Erin hinted her to wear something comfortable, so Aa got into her jogging dress. She took off the hoodie, but Baby sworn she looked sexy with it too.

"I don't want him to think I am a robber!" She shook her head front of the mirror.

"He may have never seen one like this; after all we didn't see one since we landed!" Baby shrugged.

"Well, I'll find out soon enough…" She imitated jogging to the door. She saw thru one of the security feeds that Erin just stopped by the house.

"Let's scare him!" She winked and opened the door exactly when Erin wanted to knock.

He seemed surprised when Aa opened the door. He wore a black leather jacket, beige pants and walking shoes.

"Let's go honey!" She smiled at him, touched his chest and jogged past him.

Fumbling with the keys in his hand he turned around and followed her outside.

"What is this?" Erin pointed toward her while he was driving thru the city.

"Jogging dress, don't tell me you have never seen one?" Aa tested the waters.

"Swear to never." He shook his head with belief. It occurred to him earlier that he doesn't know anything about her future plans. He had to inquire about them, but he had his own plans for today.

"Where are we going?" Aa asked coyly seeing Erin passed both downtown and his house.

"To the beach!" Erin smiled.

"Why?" She smiled.

"To be alone." Erin returned the smile.

Aa was waiting for this moment to come for a long time. However she seemed to be in trouble figuring out Erin's destination. He turned left on the rural road, away from the beaches she came to know. She voiced her concern to Erin who just waved in the air. "Most people go there. On the beach there is a huge monument commemorating the landing of the enemy on our soil... The kids are taken there every year, but we're going to the northern tip and actually we are going to hike first, hence for the comfortable shoes!" He grinned.

She touched his neck and combed thru his hair. He was occasionally very creative she had to admit.

The path led thru the hillside. Aa spotted some waterfalls and eventually they exited the tree covers and arrived to a gentle hillside that ended at the waterline. The view was magnificent - Aa concluded. She gently touched his shoulder. He pulled her closer and she didn't protest. "So how often do you seduce your girlfriends to come here?" She giggled.

"I haven't brought here anyone since my wife..." He mumbled and opened his backpack.

Aa's eyes moistened: he actually brought launch with him! He opened the blanket then rolled it out to the grass. Next he assembled the umbrella to cover them from the sun. It was so thoughtful of him, she couldn't wait him to land on the blanket, she practically pulled him down.

"Hey, what are you doing?" He frowned.

"Come on, enjoy the openness!" She laughed.

"You know, we click so well, have you ever considered staying in Akron forever?" Erin finally asked her directly. He could tell it hit a nerve, because the woman's mood darkened. "I don't know; certain things are beyond my control. However I'll try to stay as long as I can!" She smiled.

"But…"

"Baby, just leave it like that. This is such a wonderful day and I want to enjoy myself!" She smiled and kissed him. He kissed her back, holding her head in his hands. She unbuttoned his shirt ad he slightly opposed.

"Aren't you brought me here to seduce me?" She uttered into his ears.

"But what if somebody comes?"

"Loosen up, would you?" She widened her smile and kissed his bare chest.

It was late afternoon by the time Aa woke up. Erin left to get more water in about a good mile away from where he took her. She had a fantastic day so far, but now something bothered her. She couldn't figure out what it was, but the nagging feeling didn't dissipate. Something she supposed to do… No, it was something her team mates supposed to do…

Erin just refilled the two bottles from running water near the flag post and turned around to walk back on the beach when he spotted two dark spots on the sky. The two spots rapidly approached the coastline. He frowned, and hoped he would return to Aa where he left his binoculars, but of course it was impossible and he knew it. He fastened his steps and tried to hurry up. In his mind he gave thumbs up to himself; almost nobody was at the flag post, just as he expected. He considered himself to be the luckiest guy in the world and turned his attention to the sky where he saw the spots. The dark objects grew in size and he could make out their general shapes too. They were helicopters. Strange – he thought of it. Helicopters usually don't venture out toward north. There is nothing there…

Aa felt then heard the helicopters coming. The nagging feeling deepened and she stood up, facing toward the ocean. She spotted the two dark green helicopters running low, with their silencers on. She saw a binocular in Erin's backpack and grabbed it. Of course the helicopters belonged to SCC 26-54, Josh Kulighan's flagship that sailed somewhere out in the ocean and under visual cloak. She shook her head as the choppers flew past her with barely any noise other than the air whir-pooling.

Erin arrived couple minutes later. He seemed thrilled.

"Sweetheart, did you see the green helicopters?"

Aa tanked her head.

"I have never seen them before, but it's true, they exist!" He was overly excited.

She just shook her head quietly. *What a morons…*

"Hey, Aa, did you see it too?"

Aa considered denying the whole thing to him, but felt anger against Josh's master plan. Poor management from their side… She was hesitant: "I saw something, but by the time I looked up whatever they were, they were gone!"

"I'm telling you, they were the government's helicopters! They had to be because I've never seen this layout before!" Erin protested.

"If you say so…"

It was late at night when Aa returned to the apartment. Erin gave her a wet good bye kiss and she didn't protest.

"I had a wonderful day!" Erin stated.

"So did I; honey!" She caressed his face.

He blushed and bit his lip for a moment. "Two great things happened to me today! I was with you and I've seen those helicopters Aas kept talking all those years and nobody believed him, including myself!"

"You think you saw them!" Aa reminded him.

"Well… I am sure they were…"

"You believe what you wanted to believe!" She hoped to convey her skeptical attitude while exiting the car.

Once back at the apartment Aa turned to Josh and before he could pump her about some info she leashed out on him. "Let me guess, the AVD helicopter brought you the supplies while the Ka-28 Kamov was the hunter and had the electronic countermeasures pod beneath its half wings?"

"How you know that?" Diesel walked into the room amid deep frowns.

Chapter Fourteen

Ambush

Erin made breakfast for his daughter and for himself. Aa wouldn't say what her plans were or that who are those others whom might be controlling her destiny but hoped she would stay forever. In that case they would have to move to a bigger apartment and he already heard that the penthouse on the top floor was looking for new tenants…

"Well, well, Papa you have disappeared yesterday! No phone calls, no messengers! One would think you have done something grownups would do!" Zoe changed the end of the sentence. Wiped the word 'naughty' and replaced with 'grownups would do'. Just as she thought, his father smiled, hiding his true whereabouts from her. She was hoping to see Aa soon again. She was such an upbeat and electrifying person!

"Hey, hey, not for kids!" His papa shook his index finger and just poured the cereal mixture into her bowl when his beeper went off.

He looked the number and didn't recognize it, but called it anyhow.

Zoe listened into the conversation with half ears.

"Yes sir… yes and you have him! That's great news I am on my way!"

"Is anything important, Papa?"

"Yes, very important, my darling!" He kissed her while called Corporal Tok to pick him up immediately.

This time he sat beside Tok who put up the sirens and the cruiser sped toward South.

"So did the protectorate say how did they acquire him?" Tok tried to engage with his superior.

"Only that they picked him up, presumably at his sister's house. He is in protective custody. As per my request they called me personally. The Commissioner doesn't know this!"

"Is that wise?" His aide frowned.

"We are dealing with ruthless killer or killers here. It's best to keep information leaks to a minimum!" Erin was clearly worried. The picture of Aa quietly slipped into the back of his mind, the job took her place now without question.

Erin was surprised how far they had to drive to get to the protectorate's main building. It took them a good five hours on the deserted highway once they left Akron. Deserted, because the electric bubbles can't travel that far. Erin was sure of it.

He signed the custody papers, all the other pertinent release amendments and the local officers soon brought a man to him in handcuffs.

Erin frowned, but said no word. According to the receptionist he didn't protest but was seemingly exhausted.

Erin decided to watch him closely and got to the back of the car with him, while Tok drove them back.

"Mr. Alok!" Erin spoke to him after a while.

"Y...yes?" The man turned to him. He was scared. Dark pads beneath his eyes were the sure telltale signs of sleep deprivation...

"I'm police Chief Erin from Akron. I'm taking you to police custody!"

"No salvation!" He shook his head disappointed.

"From what?"

"The devil is following me! Don't take me home, please don't do it!" He begged.

Erin frowned. "I'm taking you to the precinct where I work!"

"Good!" He seemed relieved for a moment, than bit his lips. "I don't want to die!"

"You will not! Did you pick up those archeologists in…"

"Yes I did, crazy bunch of people! Late at night when everybody supposed to sleep and dream of peaceful life, but no, these were tainted by others and now the devil is after me, like after them!" He shook while he spoke.

Erin and Tok exchanged glances. This will be a difficult interrogation. This man has gone insane!

It was evening by the time they returned to the precinct where Tok completed all the remaining paperwork. Erin took Alok to the interrogation room and told the officer to start the audio and video recordings. This was a gut feeling of him after he watched Mr. Alok getting out of the car. He was beyond nervous and he only saw that in the war, when sleep deprived people would pick up on things that nobody else could, not even the radar… For a moment even Erin panicked but then he controlled himself; after all there is no devil.

On the way to the interrogation room Alok suddenly turned to him. "Listen man, they had a thing!"

"Who?" Erin asked.

"The victims! They took it from the building. They were very excited, said it's… encrypted or something. You know there were writings on this object." Alok shook just by remembering it.

"Hold your thought! Once in the room we'll sit down, get something to eat and…"

"No, no no… no time. One of them said they have to take it to a friend, a cryptologist. They said it's a lifetime's discovery and that they should document the whole thing for later, you know… Its… they said they will take notes to safe place at their house!"

"Safe?" Erin frowned.

"They wrote papers in cab…to put them away once they arrive to their home!" Alok was very worried. Erin was about to get some cheap coffee when suddenly Mr. Alok grabbed his coat: "Don't leave me alone!" He screamed after him.

Erin saw Tok running down the hallway.

"What is it?"

"The word got to the Commissioner. He wants to be present!"

"Does he realize this will push the questioning into the morning?" Erin scratched his head.

"Sir, Alok is the safest here!" Tok tried to reassure him.

"I know that! Now I have to go back and tell him to sleep in one of the cells!" He shook his head.

Of course Mr. Alok wasn't very understanding. Erin took pity on him and brought some food from the local restaurant across the street than asked Tok to drive him home.

"I was hoping to interrogate him now!" Erin disappointedly shook his head. He was still between angry and annoyed that a superior crossed over his plan.

"Sir, maybe he'll get some sleep. This could be good for us." Tok replied.

Erin winced and laid back. He was somewhat tired. Suddenly the radio began flashing. It was the Chief who saw the blinking line and alerted his driver.

Tok flicked the switch and suddenly screams and gunshots filled the air.

"What's going on?" Erin turned toward the speakers.

"They are transmitting in the open, sir!"

"Which station?" Erin had a bad feeling.

"Ours, sir!" Tok's face went pale.

"Turn the car around, now!" Erin screamed and went to check his gun in the holster.

"Do you think it's about our prisoner?" Tok apparently had the same bad feeling as Erin. He couldn't answer as the entire block ahead of them suddenly engulfed in fire and smoke.

"Go from the back!" Erin shouted. Tok turned the steering wheel hard to the right and for the moment the cruiser's tire lost contact with the ground.

Erin jumped out from the car, gun in his hand, safety off. Tok was right behind him with his own gun in his hand.

Erin felt high from the adrenalin spreading in his body... He felt the world was slowing down around him as he ran inside the building. The fire alarm was going off; smoke in every direction. The lights were on minimum; still fighting for first place on the monthly electrical savings – it occurred to Erin who found his protest against this matter well justified right now.

He checked the interrogation room, but it was empty. He walked over an officer who lay on the ground, motionless, and at the corridor junction he peeked to his left. He saw another officer on the ground, but the thick smoke obstructed his view. Tok jumped out from behind, hoping to draw fire if there was anyone hunting for them.

Erin noted his bravery and since no fire came, he moved toward the cells. The cell mates

cried, screamed and cursed inside. He took one look inside cell 13, noted the cab driver on the floor and he was running toward the front entrance to try to stop anyone leaving. He saw more injured as he got closer to the main lobby. The receptionist screamed, apparently the blast cut deep into her shoulder. Erin's mind registered the devastation as he moved out to the open. There were tire marks on the street, but he saw nobody, so he turned around and spotted Officer Harl holding his head, walking toward him.

"What's happened Harl?" He grabbed the officer.

"Soon as you guys left they came and we let them in! I mean they walked thru us! They asked where the prisoner you brought in was and we told them!" Harl grabbed the arch of the wall to hold onto something solid.

"Why did you guys tell them?" Erin didn't understand.

"It… seemed logical they want to talk to him… they said. It was the prisoner who started screaming, then one of them hit him, the others seemed confused and the prisoner just screamed more… then we woke up from this dream and everybody started shooting!" Harl had to sit down. He was still confused by the events.

"How many came in?"

"Three, no four of them, armed to the teeth and mask on their heads!" Harl was looking for some water. Tok gave him the bottle then Erin organized a search party to clear the building with other officers whom arrived from the neighboring stations. By that time the fire department and the medics arrived as well.

One of the last persons who got to the scene was Police Commissioner Rally Adams. He grabbed Erin by his coat and took him to the interrogation room himself, accusing him a lot of things and it took the logs to clear him of any association to the attack.

"This city hasn't seen anything like that since the Mossur massacre!" Adams cursed.

"What are we going to do now?" Erin was seemingly nervous. He was still under shock from the events.

"I tell you what! You found somebody important for the assassins because they came in full force... and this shit that my men let them in and showed them the prisoner? What the hell is going on here?" Adam scratched his head.

"Sir they shot all of the cameras, but we have the tapes!" Erin tried to offer some help.

Adams sat down in the chair and shook his head. "I have no idea how to explain this to my superiors and let me tell you, there are more of them by the hours!"

Erin called home, but his daughter was asleep. He left message on the answering machine - the second time he did that since he bought the damn thing - then helped with the recovery efforts. Within one hour he was watching the security tapes along with Rally Adams at his office.

"They had no electrical cables!" Erin shook his head watching one of the masked men pointing a device not larger than his own gun toward the camera and taking it out.

The coroner dropped by who was also involved in the cleanup efforts and reported that Mr. Alok is dead and he is running everything he could to determine if he was interrogated in a fashion like two of the archeologists whom had something in their bloodstreams. He also noted that the driver was killed by one shot, between the eyes, with a high powered non-conventional weapon.

"So, how long till the military arrives?" Erin turned to Adams once the coroner left.

"Actually I believe this will be taken care of another way. If you excuse me, I have to meet with the head of the Civil Defense Ministry!" Adams pointed toward the door.

Erin's jaw dropped. "I guess I don't want to be here!"

"No you don't!" Adams shook his head. He seemed tired.

Erin went down to the hall where officers and firemen worked hard on the cleanup. He wanted to help, but Tok told him to get to his car and take a rest. Erin was tired indeed. He went out like a light.

The next moment corporal Tok was knocking on the car's door. Only after sitting up and getting out of the car, did Erin notice it was dawn already! He slept for more than three hours!

"What's up?"

"The Commissioner wants to see you!"

"I guess you don't want to be in my shoes, huh?" Erin tried to crack a joke.

"Not at all, sir!" Tok seemed serious.

Chapter Fifteen

Erin became timid when he spotted the three suits sitting in the Commissioner's office.

Adams introduced him to the head of the Civil Defense Ministry, to Mr. Erdmor.

"How may I be of service?" Erin tried to suck up. The head guy looked all too clean and serious. Erin watched his spotless suit.

"Sit down, Chief!" Mr. Erdmor pushed each word like he has hard time to talk.

Erin frowned and sat down into the last, remaining and empty chair.

"Let me tell you how this going to go down Mr. Erin!" The man played with his fingers for a moment, assembling the sentences in his head and thinking it over one more time. After all he will lay his trust in the Chief and the Commissioner and if things go south, so as his carrier…

"Last night this police precinct received small arms replenishment thru the front entrance because of a civil truck blocked the back entrance. The shipment had to be unloaded within fifteen minutes upon arrival as per the code, hence the decision to unload at the front. Due to negligence on the shipper, one of the crates got loose containing grenades. One of the safety pins dislodged causing the crate to explode killing two police officers, injuring seventeen more and causing severe damage to the front of the building. The Civil Defense Ministry will honor the two fallen officers to be called as our own; therefore they will be cremated within eighteen hours of the accident.

The Civil Defense Ministry will also cover the cost of the full police and Civil Defense burial ceremony!

The following has to take place: all damaged cameras will be dismantled and transported away by a Civil Defense contractor today. The same contractor will set up and install the newest state of the art camera system, a gift from us for your troubles. Any tapes or audio recordings you may have has to be destroyed immediately, is that understood?"

"Yes, but…" Erin protested, but Mr. Adams was seemingly finished: "Our recordings failed at the attack and we are to obey all your requests to the fullest extent, isn't it right Mr. Erin?"

"Yes…" The Chief replied reluctantly, albeit a bit confused.

"Splendid, Commissioner!" Mr. Erdmore nodded.

"Why the lies?" Erin frowned.

"This investigation can go down two ways, Chief. I can take over and run an investigation regarding to police negligence of how four masked man gained entrance to the building by willingness showed by the Commissioner's staff, failure to report the first mass homicide to me and the strange interrogation techniques used presumably by the assassins or…" He trailed off.

Erin chuckled. "I am listening to the second option!"

"Good boy!" Erdmore acknowledged, then continued: "I've been watching you for some time and you've done a great service to this city. Son of a fallen police Chief of the presidential city… You've showed integrity, honor and justice from day one. If all goes well you will take Adam's seat once he retires. Now to cut to the bullshit I convinced the President to hold off the military of this investigation. This whole thing is utterly inconvenient in timing and the methods used point to perhaps a domestic terrorist group and not agents of the Land of the Aggressors. The President will soon speak to the nation, opening reconciliations to our past enemy. Fact is we have rebuilt their infrastructure in the past two decades; without us they can't exist and we need to see our investment to grow so we can harvest the results!"

"What's that mean?" Erin found this whole conversation utterly murky!

"It means, Chief that for now you will continue your investigation, but know this: I am watching you and everybody else! You must report to the Commissioner every eleven hours because he has to report to me! Frankly I don't want to see not one soldier on our streets when the President is making a speech about freedom and the prospects of the future, unity and working together! The military has a tendency of messing things up, since the last time we gave them the ignition codes of our nuclear arsenal! General Hagee gave me his personal assurances that he is holding back his horses for now."

"The war hero?" Erin's jaw dropped.

"Yes. Now frankly because of your history of following the law and your public image is excellent you are to continue until I see fit to intervene. Civilians more likely to answer for you then to an inquiry board of the Civil Defense Ministry. We don't want to create paranoia of this laser gun theory and it is my responsibility to keep this away not just from the public but from the military as well. They don't have this technology and so we must learn why we are in the interest of others. It may very well hold the key to our survival as a human race. The military would botch this like they usually do and it can lead to a catastrophe. All I can say if you guys want to see a prospective Republic then you support our President and the civilian space initiative and help finish Star City at the Koval islands. From there we will launch not just our commercial satellites but humans to space by the end of the decade!" Mr. Erdmore finished, offering his hand to both of them.

When he and his people left Erin rolled his eyes: "Man I don't know who is more paranoid; him or Aas, the radio host of PS station! Money to go to space, the biggest black hole I've ever seen!"

"Watch for your excellent public image, we need that to hold onto our jobs!" Adams warned before letting him leave the office.

"I didn't know I had one!" Erin flinched. He was tired and partially confused. It was time to go home...

The next morning Erin found his daughter in the bathroom getting ready for school.

"Where have you been, Papa?"

"Horrible things happened last night, my little girl!" Erin shook his head as he sat down on a chair in the kitchen.

"Like what?" Zoe frowned.

"See there was an accident in the police station, ammunition blew up... lots of injured and I was there until the investigation cleared me!"

"Did the boss do the investigation?" Zoe implied Adams.

"No. It was actually done by the head of the Civil Defense Ministry, by Mr. somebody..." Erin trailed off. He was tired.

"Was it Mr. Erdmore?" Zoe's eyes went wide.

"Yep."

"You met one of the most influential men of our time, you so lucky, Papa!" Zoe lit up.

"I don't think so…" Erin recollected his memory about the most inconvenient conversation in years.

"Did you know he is the one who oversees the building of the new spaceport on the Koval islands?"

"He mentioned something like that, why?" Erin grabbed a piece of bread. He was hungry too.

"I'll go there to work when I grow up!" Zoe announced.

"To be a professor?"

"I told you Papa, I want to be a scientist, an astronaut!" Zoe grabbed his shoulder and shook it, like she could just reinforce him like that.

"Yes, yes I remember now… Go to school and learn something useful!" He frowned and gently pushed her away. He was utterly tired. As soon as Zoe left he went to his room and promptly fell asleep on his bed.

"What's wrong Zoe?" Greeta approached her between classes on the hallway. Zoe seemed withdrawn, more than her usual ways.

"Papa doesn't think of much of the scientists, and I want to be one of them!" She said, her eyes misty.

Greeta knew most people don't think of them too much, but she heard they get paid well, so it was fine in her book.

"Look, it's your life! Do what you want, he'll adjust!"

"Thanks Greeta, I promise I'll get you a job wherever I going to work!" She repaid her kindness with optimistic outlook of her own.

"Are you still want to go to space?" Greeta carefully addressed the subject.

"Definitely, that's where I belong!" Zoe thought of it. "You know what? They have to communicate somehow with the planet, so you can be my dispatcher!" She brightened up.

Greeta laughed. "I don't think so…"

"You can answer the phone, right?" Zoe asked her looking all too serious for a simple chit-chat.

"Of course, but I think that is a serious job there; they not going to give it to the daughter of a runaway alcoholic!" Greeta shook her head sadly.

"Look, I tend to go with what I know and collect more while I observe the situations, we'll make it work!" Zoe suddenly blushed.

Greeta followed her eyesight and smiled. "Girl you falling for the bad guys, you need to find a nerd with glasses who study all day, not the head guy of the junior football team!"

"But he is so cute and strong!" Zoe daydreamed about the guy she was in love in school.

"Come, on, we'll be late from class!" Greeta shook her head while grabbing her best friend.

Erin woke up early afternoon and one of his first thoughts revolved around Aa. He made some strong coffee and while holding his head to stop the spinning he searched for her number.

Of course it was her father, who picked up the phone, but he sounded nice and soon he heard the honey sweet voice he was longed after.

"I heard the news in the radio, are you and your men all right?" Aa inquired, sounding sympathetic.

"I am fine, but some of my men didn't make it. As you know there were two deaths." Erin said, still unsure of how he was going to proceed with the investigation. He had to go back again to the rented house to search it again, the thought occurred to him.

"I am so sorry of that, what a stupid, freaky accident!"

"Yeah, well listen, I was wondering if you would be free tomorrow." Erin tried to change the subject as he was not allowed to talk about it too much.

"Sure, for you, any time!" She actually smiled on the other end of the line.

Erin blushed behind the phone.

"Erin?"

"Yes darling?"

"When?"

"Around nine o'clock, but Zoe will be with us too. I supposed to take her to the circus!"

"I'll be happy to tag along!" Erin heard Aa's happy voice and he loved it. He grabbed a sandwich and left with the cruiser. It was late evening when he got back home. He visited the police station, reported as he was ordered and searched the rented apartment of the archeologists without much luck. He checked the walls for hidden compartments, the ceilings and even the toilet, but he found absolutely nothing! The cab driver wasn't lying, he was sure of it… It meant he missed something and that realization pissed him off. He strived for excellence and secretly hoped to be better than his father. In cases like this he sometimes held an imaginary conversation with him, to see the crime scene with his father's eyes. What he would do different? Unfortunately the imaginary conversation didn't lead to any tangible clues while he was riding home in the night…

Chapter Sixteen

"Papa, this isn't the way to the circus!" Zoe frowned in the police cruiser's back seat as Erin made a right turn, off the main avenue.

"Aa will come along, is that all right?"

"I'll love it!" Zoe lit up. The two best persons she knew will be with her!

"I love your stylist, you work any dress!" Zoe shook her head as Aa sat down beside her in the back of the cruiser. She had a short sleeved shirt and beige man pants on her, but even with these ordinary wardrobes, she still looked superb.

"Thank you honey! See I had no money when I grew up, so I had to be creative, but later when I had money, things got more interesting, with more choices. I've got shirts for many occasions, many dresses. I love a good fabric that brings out my features!" She smiled.

Zoe giggled, she understood.

"Hey, ladies what's going on back there?" Erin frowned. He didn't hear his name, but he was sure he was somehow involved in their conversation. He would've liked if she would sat at the front with him, so he could bask in her beauty, but it also meant a lot for him that she accepted Zoe so naturally.

Aa enjoyed the circus, she has been in amusement parks near Delta city when she was dating with a fellow petty thief, but that was long time ago. She spotted a device that measures muscle power as one smacked the base with the hammer. She frowned: "I guess certain things are universal!"

"Papa is very good at it!" Zoe ran back to grab him.

Erin tried to get out of the situation, but Zoe was adamant. Aa seeing Zoe's aggressiveness added: "I'll go up against him, how is that?"

"You? This is a man thing!" Erin half frowned. Apparently he thought she was joking.

"How heavy is this thing, anyway?" Aa grabbed the hammer with both of her hand. It could've been heavier she thought as she dropped back to the ground.

Erin watched the hammer going down, then thought, 'what the heck' and went for it.

Zoe jumped in the air, she was so excited. His father got eighty five points. He rolled up his sleeves and tried again, this time for a solid ninety two. He turned around. "Your turn!"

"Okay!" Aa replied thoughtfully before grabbing the hammer. She was about to smash the damn thing when she realized, that would not be a smart move, so she actually slowed it down, still hitting a good eighty.

Erin's eyebrows ran up, he was so surprised. She didn't look that tough or strong...

Zoe turned to her rallying her cause. "You could do better!"

Aa bent forward and uttered to her: "No need to abuse the power just for showing up! Otherwise where is the surprise?"

"You are strange! You could make my Papa terminally interested in you with your talents!" Zoe replied honestly.

"I like your choice of words!" Aa squinted. She straightened out, chin high. Zoe knew she'll not try again.

Erin stepped closer, scrutinizing his girlfriend. "You don't sweat?"

Aa smiled. "It would smear my make up!"

"Sometimes you are so strange!"

"Thank you!" Aa smile widened, then thought of it half loud. "I am turning as sarcastic as Azure…"

"Who is she?" Erin inquired hearing another strange name.

"My brother's girlfriend. She broke two soldier's jaw just because she didn't like the way they talked to her…" She grimaced, apparently disliking her rawness.

"You are nothing like that!" Erin kissed her cheek. It helped Aa to mask her protest. Actually she could be just as tough as her! Just this lone thought made her feelings for Smith surface along with jealousy against Azure. She shook her head; that was another world. This is hers now and she wanted to enjoy every moment of it.

Zoe liked the big wheel and while Erin tried to show how well he took it, he actually hadn't. Aa on the other hand was always looking out of the cabin, observing and visually enjoying the situation. She noted his discomfort and figured that a little distraction would only help him, so asked of his ongoing investigation.

Erin wanted to mask his weakness from his daughter and Aa distracted his concentration so he mentioned only that he believes there was an evidence that was given to another person to figure out what it is and most unfortunately the cab driver who overheard the conversation suffered the same fate as the archeologists... All while holding to the handrail with both of his hands and grinding his teeth during the entire ride…

They watched horse trainers and a six legged creature to play with balls. Aa couldn't decide where the hell the animal lived before or how it evolved...

"Daddy, shoot the doll for me!" Zoe hugged her father by the shooting bar.

"Witch one, darling?" Erin tried to mentally prepare himself for the daunting task.

"The biggest one!" Zoe clapped her hand in excitement.

"Of course!" He frowned and paid for the mega shot. He had to hit all five sacks out of the five chances he got with a crudest handgun he saw in a long time.

He got right only two, getting his hand on an extra round of ice cream and a small doll.

"I am sorry, darling, but the weight of that pistol is so horrible! Let's get the free ice cream before going home!" He tried to cheer her up, but she was visibly upset.

"Come on!" Her father waved toward them, but Zoe was close to crying.

Aa tried to calm her down. "Look, I know you think your father is the best, but sometime things just doesn't work out right!"

"But my father is a police officer, he has a hand gun, he could've done better!"

"He isn't a solider! You should thank to whomever you pray that he doesn't know how to use it that good! He would have to carry too much weight!" She was sure Zoe doesn't understand her, but the girl nodded. "I don't want him to feel guilty about somebody else's untimely death, but I really wanted something huge!"

Aa thought of it for a moment. Flinched, she watched Erin standing in the line for the ice cream, then with a devilish mile she bent forward to meet her eye to eye. "You really want a huge doll?" Aa's eyes scrutinized Zoe's face.

"Yes!"

"All right, then!" She straightened up, walked to the booth and paid the mega shot. The woman looked at her like how the smallest wind would blow her away. She finally asked with deep disgust: "You?"

"I'll try!" Aa chirped innocently, shrugged, getting her hands on the pistol. She grimaced and turned to Zoe. "Your father was right, the weight of this is really off, and I don't think I could get the biggest doll for you!" She then spun the pistol and fired the first shot.

She felt the adrenalin taking over her senses and actually she liked to swim in it. When it was over, she had four perfect and one barely miss; it hit the edge of the container.

"How did you do it?" The booth owner asked when Aa walked up to claim her prize.

"Practice ma'am, lots of practice!" Aa replied darkly and truthfully.

Erin was walking back to Zoe's last known location while holding onto the three ice creams. He spotted a huge teddy bear nearby and frowned. He wondered who could get the biggest prize? He wanted to give it another try, he was confident he could get three baskets in, but any more was pure luck.

Aa turned around and smiled. "Look what we shot while you were away!"

Erin was speechless.

"I missed one, but the woman took pity on our soul and gave her the bear!" Aa pointed at the grinning Zoe.

Erin frowned, he didn't believe in her. Even after dropping off Aa, he asked Zoe about five times how they got the bear. Each time Zoe replied with the same story. Eventually she added. "Look Papa, she is good like that, it's her past, she has been thru a lot I think!"

"I think so too!" Erin agreed.

Chapter Seventeen

Monday morning caught Erin at the police commissioner's office. He gave his first report since Friday, but of course there was nothing to report…

The commissioner was less than enthusiastic: "Mr. Erdmore called me even on the weekend. He is persistent. I told him nothing new, but it would be time to produce something!"

"I intend to go back to the slaughter house," Erin referred to the victim's address "and go thru one more time with a fine brush!"

"That's a start!" Adams nodded, hopeful that it would turn up something they missed so he could finally report something… *So something would happen…* He then rolled his eyes. He hated to be cornered like that.

Erin was half way back to his booth when he realized, he needed to talk with the coroner. He changed his direction and went to the basement.

"I was wondering when you're going to show up!" The coroner greeted him with a piece of a computer printout.

"What is this?" Erin looked at the paper.

"Evidence of the same silicon compound I've found in the headshots."

"So he was interrogated too?" Erin looked up.

"I think so. I was wondering: you know how they came in without firing a shot and the officers upstairs didn't protest and all..?"

"What are you getting at?" Erin didn't like where the conversation was going.

"The whole thing went off in couple of minutes, I measured it!"

"And?"

"First I thought the attackers might manipulating time, but I don't think they are that powerful…"

"Well, that's good to know…" Erin frowned at the coroner.

"I mean that's what I think, but they might able to use mind control, to suppress our minds! Maybe that's how they got in."

"I don't like that thought at all!" Erin said plainly.

"Now, if they can control minds, then how come they not stopped you yet?"

Erin looked at him. "You asking all the inconvenient questions today, how come?"

"I'm just asserting this. Is it ever occurred to you Chief that maybe they are on a mission and they want whatever their objective is? If they let you, let us freely look around, this may mean they don't think of us too highly; we aren't a threat to them!"

"That would be a sad thought!" Erin concluded, but something inside of him fought for revenge, satisfaction and recognition. "I'll beat the odds!" He said openly.

"Don't die in the process!" The coroner warned him.

"Since you are running with your brown alien story so adamantly I might tell you that the head of the Civil Defense Ministry thinks the same way! I had the unfortunate luck to talk to that delusional mind on Friday!" Erin shook his head, somewhat disgusted as he recalled the conversation.

"He supposedly is a bright fellow!" The coroner lit up.

"I thought you would say that! He thinks I should keep an open mind and investigate whether his idea stands and if it does, why they are interested in us!"

"So you are on a mission, Chief!" The coroner offered his hand. Erin accepted it, not knowing if this was a joke or not.

"You think they got something out of the driver's head I don't know?" Erin was worried.

"Hard to say. It really depends on what this chemical compound supposed to do. Honestly? I don't know Chief!" The coroner shrugged.

"I'll better go now!" Erin bobbed his head and went topside to report to Adams, so he could run away. Afterward he grabbed a cigar, lighted it up and went outside where Corporal Tok was waiting for him with the cruiser.

"Where to go now?" His aide asked.

"Back to the slaughter house, I hope you packed lunch!" Erin replied, deep in his thoughts. That driver couldn't tell anything concrete and useful for him beside that the object in question was taken to a cryptologist. There had to be hundreds of them... Although Tok was conducting a formal interview with all of them, it went rather painfully slow.

Inside the apartment, they took apart all the furniture, checked the walls one more time, but found absolutely nothing. He had their files with him and he was browsing them for any clues he might missed the first hundred or so times. He lit up a second cigar and allowed the fumes to consume him. The victims were working on the city's blueprint ... *What if?*

Suddenly he jumped from the chair, scaring the Corporal.

"Sir?"

"Move that sofa to the side!" He pointed to the item. While Tok grabbed the heavy piece of furniture, he yanked the huge rug from beneath it.

"I've got it!" He smiled at the square cut into the floor. It took a moment to lift the fake cover while Tok grabbed a flashlight.

In the shallow opening was a case and a bag side by side. Erin opened the case and found some notes in it. Among them a name and an address, stating 'buddy, Welden, the cryptologist'

"We are leaving now! Call the station and ask for a backup to the above address!" Erin felt to be closer to the solution. There was a person in this city who might kno everything. It was a thrilling prospect!

He took the case with him. On the way down he opened it and found a broken clay tablet inside with scribbles on it, but it was useless for him now as he couldn't decipher the hieroglyphs.

Tok drove like a madman; they arrived in about thirty minutes later. The backup car just arrived when Erin double checked the name tag on the postal box.

"Follow me!" He hollered at the officers and ran inside the building.

"Man this is ugly!" Tok asserted the situation. He was standing beside Erin; door busted by the cops in the main living room, that used to be a living room once, before a human bomb went off inside. Everything was smashed, like if a mental institute's occupants were unleashed on it! To top off all the damage; there was blood everywhere! On the ceiling, on the walls on the books, some splattered even into the kitchen.

"Awful smell, call the coroner and the forensic team!" Erin had to get out and get some fresh air. Obviously he was on the right track, obviously whoever he is after, got here before him and they were angry this time!

"I would rather be dead by a bullet if I would have a choice!" The coroner concluded after arriving.

"Me too! Is there a way you can tell me the time of death?" Erin turned to him, fumbling with a broken glass piece.

"Sure, where is the body?" The coroner looked around the room, smiling at Erin at the end.

"I believe I saw some brain matter on the top shelf!" Erin replied sarcastically.

"Are you kidding?"

"No, no I am not!" Erin was upset and exhausted at the same time.

"Look, at least you have something to report this time!" He tried to cheer him up.

"If this is all I can report, I would rather not report anything ever again, to anyone!" Erin opened his arms in protest.

"This will take a while to mop up Chief!"

"No kidding! I guess I better inquire in the National Science Academy (NSA)!" He opened a wallet he found underneath the wardrobe.

"Another smart guy, huh?"

"Maybe if you eat his brain you'll find something we don't know?" Erin shrugged to soften his sarcastic reaction.

"That is punishable by jail, my friend!" The Coroner replied, swinging his index finger.

"At this point, anything that helps!" Erin winced. He signaled to Tok who just came back to the crime scene.

"Funny, the neighbors heard nothing!"

"Not funny at all, let's go to the NSA!" Erin replied while he pocketed the victim's valet.

The NSA was a prime example of fine government architecture. The building was built before the war. Made with real concrete, high arches at the ground and widening columns higher; it made Erin feel instantly comfortable.

He didn't have to wait for long. Like everywhere, the doors opened up for him. Sometimes he thought maybe it's because his 'public image' and sometimes maybe because of Mr. Erdmore's doing...

"Please, sit down; a tea perhaps?" The administrator offered the spicy, hot blend.

Erin tasted and like it. The blend was exotic, never tasted before. He gave a short complement and then said. "I am here because I need to ask questions about a man named Welden!"

"Professor Welden?" The administrator frowned.

"Do you know him?"

"Fairly well! He is very bright person, one of our leading cryptologists. He turned down a government job to stay in the civilian sector!"

"He should've taken the job!" Erin shook his head.

"Why?"

"Mr. Welden is dead." Erin threw the deceased's valet on the table.

The administrator took off his glasses. "That is unfortunate and troubling at the same time!"

"Tell me about it!" Erin opened his arms, up, toward the ceiling, than added: "I need his personal file and access to everything he worked on!"

"I'll get HR to compile his file today; however his work, I am afraid is classified!"

"Classified?" Erin echoed the word.

"We have government contracts and one of the key elements in those is trust. We don't speak of those in public or in private!"

"Well, that's most unfortunate. I assume you'll soon get a call from Mr. Erdmore!" Erin decided to let the system work itself for a change.

"Mr. Erdmore?!" The administrator pulled up his chair.

"You know of him?" Erin pretended to be dumb.

"Of course, the Civil Defense is a big contract!"

"Well I sort of working for him on this case, so obstructing my investigation will result a swift call from his office!" Erin drank from the tea. He had to get samples from this somehow…

"I'll see what I can do!" He punched up something in his terminal. "I think your case is very important, I don't want to obstruct Mr. Erdmore's investigation in any way!" He shook his head.

"I am glad to hear it!" Erin smiled while scooped a small amount of tea blend into his pocket.

"Let's work together on this case! I'll have another of his co-worker follow up with his logs, search for anything unusual! He taught classes here on the main campus about basic cryptology and associations. He also worked on advanced cryptographic keys, especially in the digital world."

"What's that mean?"

"Computers you know. Secure transmissions so the enemy can't figure out the commands. And if they do, they would have to commit enormous resources to decipher it on time!"

"I see!" Erin frowned. He was uneasy in this digital world; it wasn't his, he could feel it in his bones...

Erin returned to the professor's house where most of the remains were cleaned off. The coroner bagged the heavy stained books along with fragments of bones and was leaving as Erin came by.

"He died sometimes yesterday, I think! I'll give you more data once I went thru the pieces!" He lifted one of the clear bags, nodded and left.

Erin and Tok remained in the house, where he had ordered his aide to open the windows while he started to look around. He called home to make sure Zoe was all right. She assured him she left some food in the fridge and she mentioned that Aa called for him. Her name lifted his mood. He had a lot of work ahead as he sat down in one of the chairs and opened the first notebook.

Tok ran a quick errand to pick up Mr. Welden's personal files from the NSA and reported that so far they found nothing out of the ordinary in his workplace.

"I have a feeling they will not and if they do they will keep it for themselves!" Erin shook his head disgusted thinking of possible government cover-ups. He turned left and he spotted a piece of paper on top of a book shelf. He walked to the shelf and took it off. It was an ordinary paper, except the hand drawings matched one of the clay tablet he found. He put it away and asked Tok to transport him home. He wanted to take a look of the paper, but he was too tired and fell asleep after eating a cold, late, and well deserved dinner.

Chapter Eighteen

Tuesday morning Erin made sure he told Zoe in advance he was unable to pick her up from school; he anticipated his investigation to turn serious. He had no idea. While he tried to match the clay tablet to the handwritten paper in the police station, Adams called him, saying Mr. Erdmore was on his way. Little did he know the man came down to the floor to see him personally!

"Mr. Erin, how are you doing today?" Erin heard his name said as he tried to comprehend the cryptologist's possible translation about a 'Man who rules the five elements: land, sea, air, space and time. He, who guides his people to prosperity to measure up to their elders, wins their blessing beyond the light.' It made no sense to him, like no head no tail!

"Sir, what a surprise!" Erin jumped up from his chair.

"Tell me, what are you reading?" Erdmore walked around interested, to better see what he was looking at.

Of course the explanation didn't satisfy the head of the Civil Defense and it resulted, him being dragged to the Commissioner's office. He had to turn in the paper and the clay tablets, but Erin didn't mind it too much. He just amused himself with them, while he waited for the Corporal's call. Tok was at the cryptologist's house all day long.

"Let just say I'll keep these until further notice... No need to log them in!" Mr. Erdmore said behind closed doors.

"I don't like evidence being taken away from me!" Erin mildly protested. He knew he can't win, but didn't want to give it up without a fight.

"I know that Chief; hence you are leading the investigation and not someone else! By the way it was a nice touch warning the administrator of the NSA about me! Please do that in the future too if somebody stalls you!"

"You've heard it already?" Erin was puzzled.

"Good call. He needs to learn his place!" Erdmore nodded.

"Who?" Adams inquired innocently.

"The administrator of the NSA!" Mr. Erdmore turned to Adams.

"I don't like when you piss off powerful people, Erin!" Adams warned him.

"Oh no, long as I'm alive he's got my support!" Erdmore firmly touched Erin's shoulder.

"So tell me Chief, you've got some news about the investigation, beyond the death of the professor?"

"Sorry sir, nothing else. The coroner is analyzing the remains, my aide is going thru the house as we speak and I might join him tomorrow if he finds nothing, but if the assassins were after the items this clay print was made from, they may very well get what they wanted and we will not hear from them ever again!" Erin theorized.

"I need to talk to the Chief alone!" Erdmore apologized to Rally Adams.

The Commissioner nodded, and left the office, while scrutinizing Erin's face. The Chief crossed his arms. "What's wrong?"

"He doesn't need to hear what I have to say to you, but I urge you to stay on course! What you said could be true, but I don't think so. No, I firmly believe that isn't the case!"

"Care to elaborate?" Erin frowned.

"What I am about to tell you isn't for anyone else's ears, do you understand me?" He took out an immensely small device from his briefcase and placed it on the table.

"What's that?" Erin leaned forward.

Mr. Erdmore activated the device that emitted the sound of a waterfall.

"It is a crude device for distorting our voices, but I doubt it will matter if the enemy we dealing with as sophisticated as I think! See just as the police, the NSA, the military and every major company, university and government agencies, we are utilizing computers to work, to store and to retrieve information. I know you not literate, hence the way I am explaining the situation. At home you may have a computer to type up things, play a game or do math on it. At work we store vast amount of information in digital form…"

"Like how we have the Motor Vehicle database to associate names, addresses and vehicle information!" Erin nodded.

"Excellent. So we have our own information just as the police, the NSA and every other big business. Now we are also working with the NSA and the military to establish a parallel system that is connected, so we can share and analyze data immediately. No need for messengers to shuttle the magnetic cores around, less chances for something go wrong. Now the reason for real secrecy in this room comes from the fact, that the Civil Defense Ministry was hacked several times last week.

"Hack?"

"It means a person or more opened the door to a locked house to look around!" Mr. Erdmore explained.

"Why don't you report it to us then?" Erin made a loose connection between the entering into a locked house and the diligent work his men were doing keeping the public safe at all times...

"It's not a good idea. The public could lose faith in the Civil Defense Ministry. Then again, the cops don't have a cyber-forensic team, while the NSA is in the midst of establishing that right now!"

"How could they enter into your network?"

"Good question, Chief! I believe they accessed the information by getting into one of our facilities. Now, I made some inquiry thru a private contractor to give us a copy of the police mainframe logs. My team determined that the police was hacked too. They've got their hands on database information, like addresses. At this very moment my personal aide is in the NSA to consult with the administrator so we could take a peak in to their logs. My bet, they were being hacked too!"

"Why?"

"The assassins you are after are very clever, I think. They have to use our resources to find whatever they after it, and they are working on it!"

"Serious accusations, don't you think?"

"Of course! They would go away forever if we could catch them, but we have to be very lucky for that. I hope that you'll get a phone call from the NSA either way within twenty four hours, and I hope they have favorable news for you!" Mr. Erdmore picked up the device from the table and turned it off.

"Mr. Erdmore, I was wondering, if we all come out of this alive, you could do a favor for me?"

"I am listening." Erdmore tried to read Erin's face.

"My daughter is very interested of that spaceport on the islands and I was wondering if it becomes public, you might be able to arrange a tour for her?" Erin decided to ask to see how far he can get with his new and powerful contacts, more than to help his daughter. At the same time she might realize how far she is from space and give it up for good...

"I can do better than that, Chief! As soon as this is over I'll contact you and I will give her a private tour. Is she smart like that?"

"I think so, but she has dreams, like going to space and such nonsense..."

"If she is smart, healthy, she has a shot! We need dreamers to make them come thru and their dreams will be their children's reality! Good day, Chief and don't forget to report in!" Mr. Erdmore lifted his hat as he walked out of the office.

"What were you two talked about?" Adams walked in a second later.

"He is more lunatic that I thought, boss! I'll go to the professor's house to look around!"

"Maybe it's over, now that they found whatever the professor had, whatever the archeologists gave him!"

"I don't think so!" Erin shook his head with a sour smile.

Chapter Nineteen

Aa decided to take initiative and went to pick Zoe up. She had two good reasons to leave the house. The first was the fact that she was worried about the young girl the second was that Josh urged her to get more information one way or the other. She suspected some advancement in the case herself, since Erin was busy in the past two days. She had Baby to drop her off front of the school and waited patiently until Zoe appeared with Greeta.

Greeta looked both ways on the street before leaving the school's entrance. She was worried if the two girls would show up for a payback session. She spotted them coming from across the street but suddenly they stopped and turned around.

Greeta frowned, than spotted Aa. She smiled. "Hey, I know you!"

"Hey girls!" Aa smiled at them.

"How come you showed up?" Zoe asked.

"I figured I can still pick you two up, even if your Papa can't!"

"Well, then I should go on my way!" Greeta winked at Zoe.

"Are you sure?" She hoped she would tag along, but knew Greeta had to go home to do work around the house, so they hugged and went separate ways.

"Tell me something Aa, are you an angel?" Zoe asked her while walking home on the busy streets.

"Why would you say that?" She looked at her.

"Dress so sexy and look so right, you must be an angel to take notice of my father and me!"

Aa swallowed hard, eyes misty. "I see a lot of me in you. You know, the what ifs."

"No. Care to explain?" Zoe was lost.

"What if I had a good childhood? What if I had stayed in school and not ending up on the streets? What if...?" She bit her lips.

"I don't see the results of any hardship on your body!" Zoe frowned.

"Because I am a tough cookie!" She laughed.

"I knew that!" Zoe giggled.

Once back in the house Aa helped her to do some homework she understood. Later Zoe turned on the computer and showed her some of the pictures she scanned in from the family album. She also showed new star pictures she got from her science teacher. Aa took a genuine interest in everything she showed. Zoe knew Aa was strange, special somehow. She was trying to become her friend, and she voiced her discovery: "I told you I see a lot of me in you and all those ifs... I, all in all I met your Papa before I met you. He was so handsome standing on the street with a cigar that I wanted to hang out with him!"

"Don't hurt him, he likes you!" Zoe said thoughtfully.

"I know!" Aa nodded.

"Is it appropriate to ask what are your intensions?"

Aa frowned. "Intensions about what?"

"About us?"

"Well, I don't know what the future brings, but I know this; you are special!" Aa pointed at her.

Zoe turned her head away. "What do you mean?"

"You know it, I know it! I think if you meet the right people at the right moment you might become one of the most important scientist of your time!"

"Sometimes you so scare me!" Zoe shook her head. "Well I have to cook something for dinner, Papa will be tired. He works so hard lately!"

"Yeah, I noticed." Aa agreed and went to help her.

Erin just sent Corporal Tok home for the rest of the day. He looked into his report and noted that he found absolutely nothing. As tired as he was, he drove home and once in the house, he took off his coat, hat. He noticed the light coat on the coat rack and frowned. He smelled the exotic perfume and smiled: Aa was here somewhere. Erin found the girls in the kitchen, putting the final touches on a great looking dinner.

"I am surprised!" He noted her presence.

"I had to meet the specialist!" Aa pointed to Zoe, who smiled.

"I am glad you are here and watching over my little wildflower!"

Aa smiled and kissed him passionately.

He was about to inquire as of why is he so lucky when his beeper went off. He scoffed at the device and called the unknown number.

The conversation was short and Erin hung up in a minute.

"Was that the boss, Papa?" Zoe inquired.

"No, this was a different one! Not unexpected after all, but somebody is working his magic in overtime, because I only expected this call tomorrow!"

"Do you have to go in?"

"Oh no! This can wait; they found something but they are running some computer work to make sure they are being right!"

"Is this about the investigation you are on?" Aa asked seriously.

"Yes! More deaths. Well, that happened yesterday we think. This time a cryptologist was the victim. Poor soul received something from the archeologists that had strange writings on it!" Erin was tired of the complicated case.

Aa decided to give him a short massage.

"Mmm I can like this!" He lay back in the armchair.

Aa suddenly kissed his neck and playfully bit into it. Erin was alert in no time. "What are you doing?"

"Nothing honey!" She kissed him again than said her good byes. It was solid nine o'clock and Baby Haas was waiting for her on the street.

"When will I see you again?" Erin asked with a deep voice.

"It's up to you!" She smiled at him, hinting at the endless possibilities.

"How about tomorrow evening for a dinner?" Erin flashed his winning smile.

"Fine by me!" She grabbed his butt before leaving.

"Papa, you seem to be in dispersion!" Zoe giggled over his father who sat at the morning table with two forks and the morning tea...

Erin frowned and shrugged. "Oh well, I'll just call the Corporal for the car!" He was about to get up, but Zoe seemed to be taken back. "What is it?"

"You have the car!"

"You're right!" He realized.

"Is everything all right?" Zoe was worried.

"Yes, yes just my mind is preoccupied now." He tried to push Aa's image away to concentrate to his hard day.

He almost ran over a pedestrian on his way to the NSA.

Tok called him saying he'll be in the office typing up yesterday's report, so Erin walked into the building, alone. He showed his badge to the receptionist who asked him to hang around. As soon as he sat down into one of the comfortable, padded chairs a security guard appeared and asked to be followed.

The Administrator welcomed him and as he sat down he realized that the tea blend was still in his pocket from the other day. That however didn't stop him to scoop some more there!

"See Mr. Erin the ugly truth is whoever you are after seems to be all too powerful and good... I will cut to the chase since Mr. Erdmore told me that you're in the loop: The NSA was hacked last week and this week again! I had set up a makeshift forensic team that is currently working alongside with the Civil Defense Ministry. I've obtained a copy of certain logs of the police mainframe, here." He gave him a few papers. Some lines were bolded by a marker.

"What shall I look for?" Erin frowned. This digital stuff again...

"Unauthorized entries at odd times. It's unauthorized because the officer was among the dead ones from that unfortunate accident late last week! They accessed your electronic report and obviously had advantages over you because your suspect, the cryptologist was dead by the time you reached him! Even more troubling that they knew you were transporting the cab driver from the country side to the police precinct because we intercepted their crude hack at that time!"

"I'll push for paper files only from now on!" Erin was serious.

"That will not happen, Chief!" The administrator shook his head sadly. He understood Erin all too well.

"Is this why you called me here, and what is all about the tough security?"

"I try to protect myself because I know too much already! Now about the reason! As I have said the NSA was being hacked as well. What we uncovered is... troubling to say the least." He trailed off.

"Why the hesitation?" Erin frowned.

"We are considered partly government owned, actually by the Interior Ministry so technically you have no jurisdiction here. However because of your special association with Mr. Erdmore this time you may exempt from this restriction. There are many secrets among these walls. Some are secret to the outside world, and some are secrets even to the faculty here. When I saw that they hacked in to the police database with credentials from a fallen officer the thought occurred to me if they've done the same thing, and they did, hence the beefed up security. What we know right now is that about a day ago somebody logged in here, in this building with the now deceased Mr. Welden's information. The intruder accessed classified information and attempted to erase his tracks. We are trying to reconstruct the data but they've done a terrific job and we never done anything like this before!"

"So what you're saying is that you don't know what they were after, but might find something because they erased their tracks?"

"Precisely!"

"When will I be able to gain more information?"

"Please give us another day, tomorrow morning or mid-day. I'll let the professor in charge know to expect you!"

Erin was not helped out what so ever. It made no sense what so ever to him why would someone kill eight plus people, cause explosion at a police station just to get something off from a computer. He went to see the Corporal who told him to report in with the Commissioner, so he changed direction to see the coroner first. He said he found traces of the silicon compound there too. Not in a significant level, but was able to provide a precise time of the death, allowing him to send the Corporal back to the cryptologist's apartment to question the neighbors again.

"Tell Mr. Erdmore, he was right!" Erin shouted toward Adams.

"In what way?"

"This leads to the digital world and I am at the mercy of some techno mumbling crowd at the moment!" Erin shook his head, clearly disgusted.

"Why don't you go home early, Chief and have a good night rest?" Adams studied his face.

"You sure? I have to finish off the report first!"

"Finish it, then go home, call me tomorrow if you not here by noon so that I can report something back to your beneficiary!"

Erin flinched at the word 'beneficiary', and then left.

Chapter Twenty

Aas drank his energy drink as he walked to the park. As a successful host, he still considered himself as a reporter, and a very good one. Number one for a successful reporter was the proper handling of different sources, insiders, so he regularly kept in touch with them. His contact was waiting for him on the bench. He sat down, took out a small bill and moved toward the man. He supplied information that seemed reliable before.

"I heard at the Research Ministry that they seem to found an inconsistency in the top ten meters of the ocean; East from our main island." The man said.

"What kind?" Aas frowned. This was new.

"The research craft maps the oceans, take pictures of the currents. Their weekly results are uploaded to the Research Ministry's mainframe that randomly matches it against a block of underwater sound and current recording."

"I thought the project was abandoned a decade ago!" Aas was surprised.

"Yes, waste of energy to power the mainframe, but since technology evolved, they brought it back to do random checks. This is of course just a run-up to properly calibrate the first research satellite they are building."

"So what seems to be the inconsistency?"

"There are currents picked up by the underwater sensor net, but there is no visual matching of this. The spy plane will take out the camera with the best resolution available and will do temperature and broad spectrum of light readings as well."

"Do they think it's a small vessel or a submarine?"

"They are unsure at this point. The inconsistency is rather a large, unused area. The Republic has no known vessels of this size. Some thinks the Land Of Aggressors might try to use hot air balloons to spy on us, but it could've crash landed in the ocean!"

"Interesting, keep me posted! Any news on the dead people with a hole in their heads?"

"No. Maybe next week. The police are in the dark!"

Anything else?" Aas hurried up.

"Yes. There were sightings of deep green helicopters in the northern tip of this island last week."

"Any pictures or videos?"

"None. They had no sound but my source tells me that small bags and men were dropped to the island, perhaps agents!"

"I told you before, this helicopter thing is getting too old. The public wants to see or hear them and no computer generated fakes please! They are below my and my listener's taste!" Aas tapped his palm against the wooden bench.

"Same time next week!" The source walked away unassumingly.

Aas watched him leaving. This was a good time to meet. Between rush hour and the end of the shifts people were usually at home to change and the city became practically deserted. Nobody came as they were talking. He looked up to the magnificent trees. They were the kind that opened up at the top, covering the park, leaving almost no way to see the blue-green sky. Suddenly a silhouette flew across the openings of the tree leafs. He saw nothing but a dark murky object.

"What the...?" He uttered and jumped from the bench. He felt the blood rush to his brain and ran toward the canopy openings. He saw another dark spot moving swiftly on the sky. This was no imagination! His heart throbbed under his chest and he stopped behind the last tree before the small grassy field; one of the many in the large park. His eyes were glued to a spot, just above the tree line. Two, dark, green helicopters levitated above the field, ropes hanging almost to the ground and three people were going down on them. The most surreal in the whole thing was that the helicopters emitted almost no sound at all. Yes there was an ever present purring, but not the usual ear popping tak-tak-tak's.

His hands were moving slowly into his pocket, but most unfortunately he left his camera at home. '*Stupid me*!' Aas hardened his fist. The three person landed as the sun went down and the park went dark.

The ropes were pulled back, the helicopters took off like fighter jets of the war and their payload disappeared among the trees.

Aas's mouth was dry. He felt like he was on drugs as he remained on the park's trail and ran toward the presumed agents.

He hid behind some bushes and watched as the two male and one young female was talking facing away from him. He felt relieved; they had no way of seeing him that way. They had street clothes on, no uniforms. They had to be sleepers... He thought of it.

He observed them, their moves. They seemed to be discussing something. The taller man turned around. He seemed uncomfortable, looking all the directions, searching for anything that moved no doubt. Aas saw as the shorter man finally walked away, the others followed him closely. Aas knew he had to follow them. He felt the rush again in his mind; he felt like a hunter and after seeing them disappearing at the sharp bend he lurched forward and picked up the pace. He saw only two of them once he made the turn and wondered what happened to the other one, when suddenly he felt a particular object pushed against his back. Firmly, but without any doubt he recognized as a pistol. His legs went numb, his mouth dry, he started to sweat. He was stupid to think he can watch them undetected…

"Why are you following us?" The male voice with strange accent asked him.

"Why are you here? What agency are you? I saw the helicopters!" Aas replied, looking straight forward with his stiffened back.

"We are not here!" The man from behind uttered into his ears.

"Then whom is the one who pushing the gun to my neck?" Aas inquired.

"Smart ass" The man behind him replied, then slowly removed the object. Aas felt relief; maybe he won't end up in the morning newspaper's obituary section.

"Remember, we are everywhere, yet we are nowhere!" The man uttered into his ears in a way Aas lost track of time. By the time he realized nobody stood behind him, the trail was empty! He shivered and while he was utterly scared he ran toward the underground station to find comfort among other citizens.

Chapter Twenty One

Sex toy

Erin used the time to sleep until his daughter came home. Then he spent some time with her before taking a lengthy shower and left to pick up Aa. Zoe was so thoughtful, she reminded him to pick up some flowers to commemorate their first date. On his way he listened at the radio where on the PS channel Aas talked in length about some strange water currents near the coast line the hydroponics system picked up some time ago...

He knocked on the door and waited. Suddenly the door opened and she appeared in a deadly red dress.

"Hi sweetness!" He managed to say and quickly presented the flowers.

"What's going on there?" He heard an unfamiliar male voice and soon a young man, he never seen before peeked out. He made his logical conclusion and said. "You're must be Aa's brother, Smith!"

The man seemed surprised. "That would be me!"

"My name is Erin; I don't know how much Aa had said about me!" Erin introduced himself, while offering his hand.

"Well, she hides well, all her private life!" The brother managed to say something.

Diesel approached the door and Erin nodded toward him. "Don't worry sir, I'll bring your daughter back in one peace, I promise!"

"Of course, Chief!" Diesel replied.

"Honey?" Erin heard another unfamiliar female voice closing on them. A young girl with deep brown hair and matching almond eyes in extremely deep cut V necked top and black leather pants approached the brother and kissed him, while hugging him tight. Sure he'll remember her for a long time!

"We have to go!" He sensed strange urgency in Aa's voice as she practically pushed him out to the hall.

*

"I don't like when you talk about my brother like that!" Aa replied to Erin who named Smith's mistress as a 'sex toy'

"I am sorry, but I fail to see how your brother could be so different in taste like you are!"

"She may look like a tramp but she loves him, I know that!" Aa defended Evan Smith.

They were finishing their dinner at the prominent restaurant; Delicatesse of Akron, where they ate once before. He took her there as a sort of an anniversary. They met exactly three weeks ago…

"Zoe sends this to you!" He pushed a folded paper over the table to her.

Aa opened the paper and her eyes turned misty. The picture depicted a blue planet and three beings: Erin's daughter in the middle, she on the left and Erin on the right. Above them flew a crude rocket.

"She is a beautiful being, I so love her!" She folded the paper and put it into her purse.

"Strange that you say it that way, but I love you anyway!" Erin paid the bill with cash and offered her coat before they walked out, into to the busy night.

"I don't want to intrude, but your brother seemed shocked to see me! Is everything all right?"

"He was more shocked that I date with a police officer, that's all!" Aa replied.

"Why is that?"

"I told you before; we came from the Southern Demilitarized Zone. Police are very corrupt there and Smith had the unfortunate thing to go up against one. He sent me and the so called 'sex toy' away before he and his team met with the Controller. He is the guy who owns the district we lived in. Azure, the 'sex toy' was sent away with another being so to speak and Smith sent me to work with the Admiral, an old military guy who used to be the superior of our parents. Smith never returned and I and his friends, including the Admiral knew nothing of him, of my father, Diesel... Until Azure showed up one day stating she is going to defy the whole galaxy and she will rescue him. She asked our help. Everybody turned her down, even me. I had a good life along with the Admiral by then. But she persisted and went ahead anyway. By the time the Admiral organized a rescue attempt she already wrecked the Controller's assets. She rescued him. That little so called 'sex toy!' So if you have anything negative about her, keep it to yourself!"

"I am sorry, I didn't know!" Erin was shocked. He knew there were dark secrets in her past, but nothing like that.

"So, on the note of intruding, how is your investigation coming along?" She popped the question.

He frowned. Now he was obligated to tell her something, to placate her. "My team had little luck so far. The evidence I was telling you about is gone. All the leads point toward the cryptologist's workplace; the National Science Academy. If somewhere, there I might find new clues…The forensic team suggests the killers were attempting to access the internal computer network to get some data, but what was accessed isn't available yet. They tell me the system is slow, and the intruders attempted to erase those marker or index files potentially stopping our recovery efforts. You know I don't understand many of these computer stuff, heck probably Zoe understood more than I am! The only good thing comes out if this that my team can move on to the next location, the police cordon will be lifted tomorrow morning from the killers first location! Things slowly return to normal and everybody likes that except me, who can't catch those bastards."

"So you will take up residence in the NSA now? Zoe would want to tour the building!" Aa smiled, envisioning the young girl's enthusiasm.

"You think it's a good idea?" Erin wondered.

"Of course! She would love it!"

"Perhaps you could come with us too? Please!" He almost begged.

"All right!" Aa agreed.

Erin found Aa waiting for him at the entrance of their building. Little did he know Smith took the rest of her 'entourage' to snoop around the house the archeologists were found dead, where Erin's own investigation started, where he met Aa…

Erin's mighty police cruiser pulled to the curbside. She heard the breaks and turned toward the car. She smiled instantly and walked up to the rear doors to get in the back seat, to chat with Zoe along the way.

"It's so nice you came!" Zoe giggled.

"Just for you, honey!" Aa winked at her.

"I am not even in the car!" Erin uttered while his aide navigated the huge, prewar car thru the maze of streets. The local Paranoia Station program blasted from the radio. As a morning sensation commentator Aas was explaining the strange water readings then went on with the deep green, noiseless helicopters.

"Oh, come on, that's old news!" Erin dismissed the host.

"My father loves conspiracies!" Zoe admitted to Aa.

"Yeah, my loved ones, especially when the guy's name almost the same as Aa's! And those deep green helicopters... I would love to see one of them from truly up close, unlike those on that beach we keep disagreeing on!" He smiled at Aa than to his aide who agreed, by nodding repeatedly.

"Be careful what you wish for!" Aa replied with a tad of seriousness in her voice.

"Why, that I might find out that our own government really screws us?"

"No. Maybe you would find your beliefs are all but crushed. You would be very lonely after that!" Aa answered darkly.

"You know something? Have you seen anything like that down in South?" Erin read Aa's facial impressions and felt her seriousness was real.

"No, but I heard things..."

"He said he saw two helicopters just yesterday landing three agents in the northern park around dusk!"

"What?" Aa shook for a moment. She tried to mask her shock, but Zoe detected it. She looked at her and she felt cornered. "Does he have pictures or movies?"

"No, he said he had nothing with him!"

"Well then, he had no news again!" Aa put up a mental note to possibly meet this Aas before she leaves and send him to a mental facility forever, but added loudly only that too much paranoia can be dangerous.

"Wow, this is huge!" Zoe surveyed the tall, grey building. The National Science Academy had four campuses, employed more than five hundred teachers. Over ten thousand students studied every day among the walls.. It had its own helipad and research helicopter and it was said that the top science students were all recruited for the Republic's infant space program.

The mainframe's fastest terminal was located on the fourth floor, deep inside the complex. They were told that the mainframe's origin lie deep underground and way in the past. They hinted that they had contracts with the government, even before the civil war. Their guide was a senior student, a future astronomer. He was overly excited about everything technical and electronic in the NSA annoying Erin a lot.

"Here we are! This is the astro-lab. The terminals are located there and my professor will explain our recovery efforts so far!" He announced.

Erin introduced Zoe and Aa to the professor who started explaining that so far the recovery effort failed.

"Why?" Erin growled.

"We have managed to recover as much as we can and placed into the memory core, but it's incomplete. We wrote a program to extrapolate given the data available, but so many possibilities exists we don't know the answer yet!"

The professor brought up the program to the screen and of course Erin had no clue what was going on. Aa learned yesterday from Smith himself about the true reasons of them being here, looking for something an old UNHL research team made over two decades ago. She was horrified after learning what was at stakes and she figured she'll put her mind into good use by helping speeding up Erin's investigation. She decided to change history so Aa moved closer to the screen and after a while said: "Stop!"

"Why?"

"This is wrong, change that equation!" She pointed to a specific point on the screen.

"Ma'am, this is a complex high level mathematical calculation, do you have any degree in integral math and theoretical science?"

"Let me fill in for you! After you compiled and ran it gave you an error about seventy three percent? Am I right?" Aa simply cut him off.

"How do you know?" The professor's jaw dropped.

"Change that then ran the compiler. I hope the mainframe is parallelized or it will take forever!"

"What is the compiler?" Erin asked quietly behind them. His daughter walked up to him and uttered: "That's a translator. It translates this program to the code of the machine so it can work with it…"

"Thank you!" Erin scratched his head. She really knows more than he does. He felt alone for a moment.

"Of course it parallelized; one hundred and twenty eight processor works in unison with twelve in reserve in case some goes bad."

"Modular, huh? How many bits?"

"Sixty four of course!" The professor replied proudly.

"Not that bad, I hope you can delegate the tasks at least to the terminals of this building if you must! I doubt you have programs to run on people's home computers if the situation requires it. You know, download the program and let its copies work with packets downloaded from central servers…"

"That had never occurred to me!" The professor's yaw dropped.

"Better, because that is the shape of things to come!" Aa replied all darkly and serious, then walked away to check out a cool table with the solar system on its display. Zoe was playing with it and zoomed out to see the universe.

"So you want to go to space?" Aa turned to the girl.

"Of course! Maybe there are aliens and they want to talk to us. Maybe we want to talk to them just as you said it before?" She implied on an earlier conversation when they met face to face the first time.

Erin decided to approach his stunning girlfriend. She never said anything about her knowledge of this field.

Zoe saw his fast approaching father and turned to Aa. "Do you think there are smart aliens out there?"

Aa bent down to Zoe's level and touched her head. "Honey the universe is full of aliens, we just not that interesting to them, yet! I hope you'll change that!" With that statement she kissed her forehead.

Zoe turned quiet. She was shocked from the beautiful woman who would say something deep like that. Then she remembered of the drawing his father must've given to her.

"What are you two talking about?" Erin smiled at his daughter.

"Aliens and green helicopters!" Zoe replied, giggling toward Aa.

The professor called for Erin and he left, leaving the two females alone again.

"Aa, you think there are aliens in these solar systems? Close to us?" Zoe pointed to the flat screen. It took Aa a second to recognize the small planetary system of Gnem and Danal IV. The description and visuals were rather poor and she knew Emperor Acknull would be offended to learn that others present his planet as a barren wasteland. She pointed to Danal IV: this planet is more like ours, wrong colors!"

"But it's so far away! A lifetime to travel, to find out if you were right or not!" She replied.

"Don't have to go all the way to find out how it looks or to communicate with them! You can do it from space, from orbit! That way the air and dust would not obscure the view. Have a radio telescope or a highly sensitive super cooled infrared and you good to go!" Aa replied.

"You so smart!" Zoe concluded.

"You too!" Aa patted her shoulder.

*

"So I heard you were mentioned on the radio this morning!" Aa bugged Smith once she was dropped off by Erin and Zoe before the aide took them home.

"What?" Smith and his accomplices found nothing useful in the archeologist home. The police took everything already.

"A guy named Aas was on radio PS this morning talking about two helicopters, a day before in the northern park. Three agents were dropped from the noiseless helicopters!" She grinned toward him.

"Great…" Smith tanked his head.

"Maybe we can show him around on the Trixec or something. That guy really annoys me!" Diesel commented.

"Great, now we are aliens who abducting humans! No! Diesel, how much do you know about this society. Ministries and so on…?"

"Not too hard to find out, why?"

"Let's pose as a secret agency like Interior Ministry or something and check out the dig!"

"I need some time to set that up and I need help!"

"You've got us, remember? Minus Aa, who should hang out with the Chief!" Smith reminded him.

Chapter Twenty Two

Aa tried to be helpful by setting up credentials the following day, since it wasn't until later when Erin supposed to pick her up. It became a rather normal routine for her to spend the afternoons and evenings with Erin and Zoe. It gave her plenty of time to help Smith and give some reports on the Chief's investigation, but not on his private life. Smith seemed to understand her necessity to compartmentalize her private life from her investigative work and she appreciated him for that. Aa felt relieved and worried at the same time, since he never said whether he approved this stint or not. In the meantime Zoe told her bits and pieces about the society and how things work around here. She found surprising similarities between the two societies; for example human greed and the quest to save money. Erin explained vividly how he cut the stakeout on the dig where the UNHL team worked long ago. He told her in the evening that the police tape remains to thwart off the interested minds until they decide to take it off for good, but in the meantime it still count as a police presence, so they can log it as such, but costs the department practically nothing. Erin implied something like showing the police district to be more efficient than others, to be on the top of some kind of public list. Aa concluded there must be some rivalry among the stations, but when Erin left, Zoe laughed and told her about the public lists of the city of Akron. Allegedly every public and governmental building was on it. It was updated monthly and it communicated to the public just how efficiently did they operate. Her father's story fit right in, because saving money was a sure sign of being efficient...

Zoe summarized the best: "My father is a team player out of no other choice, but necessity to survive. He thinks all that efficiency and saving electricity at night by cutting on emergency light in the fire and police stations are just a cover up for our leaders to pocket the difference."

"What do you think?" Aa frowned.

"I know Papa's boss, Mr. Adams. He is crooked in a way to getting my father to play along to get to the top of those public lists any way they can, but he isn't greedy! He isn't pocketing the money and saving more natural resources keeps our air clean and perhaps conserves our world for future generations as well!"

"Interesting!" Aa replied, not elaborating further. Zoe was the future...

The next afternoon Zoe and Aa rode the public transportation system together, after she went to pick her up from school.

Zoe mentioned to her she would like to learn some deterrence tactics from a pro. Aa had to frown. Once on the bus, she pointed out signs of odd behavior or prying eyes from other passengers. Apparently it occurred to Zoe that her companionship might be an agent or spy, so she quietly asked her once they get off the bus.

Aa laughed in response. "No honey, I wish, but no I never was. Maybe I will, but no I am not!"

"But you could be one!" Zoe stressed it.

"Sure I can change the course of my life, but I am fine where I am now! While I'm not a genius, I am respected and I make my father proud!"

"I don't follow!" Zoe was lost.

"Look, I was told that geniuses often pick up something to play on, like a flute or a piano. It helps them to relax and according to a guy I know, it also helps him to see the pattern of a music being played out in life!" She of course thought of Gabriel, who was the captain of Smith's second personal space faring ship that was destroyed some time ago. While Gabriel wasn't a genius he was born in tube, being the reflection of that space faring ship's Artificial Intelligence. After the loss, part of himself he roamed the galaxy with others and learned to play the piano. He trailed Smith and arrived with him two days ago. He recently shared his discoveries of the great beats of life he feels nowadays...

"Are you playing on any instrument yourself?" Zoe asked.

"Not unless you count in fencing" She shrugged. She had to learn it as Smith expected all of the women around him to know how to fight with it and it's also a pre requisite for the Honor Guards position.

"No wonder you were good stopping that knife!" Zoe nodded, remembering back when she stood up for her and for Greeta on the street.

Aa smiled and pointed toward a candy shop on the street where they were walking. "Do you want something?"

"Sure!" Zoe lit up. She had a sweet tooth...

When Zoe and Aa opened up the door, the smell of freshly cooked food instantly hit their senses. They both frowned as they walked in and spotted Erin in the kitchen cooking something delicious. He bobbed his head toward them. "Surprise!"

Zoe and Aa glanced to each other and sat down to the table to eat.

"I had some luck at my job today, so I decided to share my happiness with the two most beautiful things I know in my life!" He announced then explained over dinner how the professor at the NSA made headway based on Aa's instruction. They were able to get the index files back and they were doing the cross referencing now. It seems the intruders were interested in blueprints only...

He did not reveal to the girls that it made no sense for him. He truly had no clue why somebody killed so many people just to get a blueprint of the pre-war Akron. Later that evening when he took her home, he asked if she would like to spend the next day with them.

Aa smiled and kissed him. He was so nice to her even if he had odd ideas of the future and it wasn't about his persistent questions whether she would consider moving in with them either... She appreciated his thought of not allowing her to take a cab or the streets at night to get home, but rather driving her home and making sure she gets into the building safely before leaving. All in all, she concluded, he was a good hearted man. It sometimes hurt her that she had to spy on his work, but she had to remind herself of Smith and that it should not affect Erin's work. She'll miss him once they off this planet and she knew it. She became attached to him and to his daughter, more than she was willing to admit it. Sometimes she dreamed of taking them with her, but of course it made no sense. They had a life here and she realized Erin wouldn't cope with a home among the stars at all. Rather than to hurt herself, she put the whole idea into a mental box and closed it.

Erin watched the woman of his heart disappear behind the doors and he took off. She was a strange, sometimes such a confusing woman. The most beautiful one he ever met and so independent. He gathered from Zoe, they click well and his daughter enjoyed spending time with her. He wondered about her strange family relations; starting with his father and his brother. Sometimes he wondered what her father was doing for a living... *Judging by the sparsely decorated room, probably not much.* She should be much happier in his house, living with a real family. He also considered her brother to be a bad influence, his girlfriend being a tramp or not! He knew that there was more to it then what she revealed and it bothered him, she wasn't fully sharing...

He tried to tell her that he would take good care of her no matter what, but it seemed that was not enough for her. She made some feelings surface inside him, he thought he forgot long ago, and he wanted her and nobody else. Erin felt sad in a way as he drove home.

Zoe was asleep already, so he sat down on the sofa in his room, turned on the vision set and grabbed a cold drink from the small table. He tried to remember to his father, to his mother, try to draw a parallel between their and his life, but they were disconnected long time ago; he lost the threads after a while...

He thought of the case he was working on; how his father would continue dodging bullets as superiors tried to turn the 'profit' toward their way. It made no sense of what so ever to kill nine people over a blueprint he concluded, but knew it had a lot to do with his case and with his father's death as well. *What if they were looking for something they didn't find in the dig?* Perhaps the city's blueprint would help them figure out what buildings survived the war or what buildings... - He fell asleep before he could come to a final conclusion on the subject.

Chapter Twenty Three

He was up early in the next morning. He cleaned up from the evening before and made breakfast. As his daughter pointed out it has to be a beautiful day as there were almost no clouds in the deep blue sky; surely a positive sign! Zoe was up early too. She knew his Papa was taking a day off to be with them. They went together to pick up Aa who wore a stunning white dress for the occasion.

After the loss of his wife Erin wanted to commit suicide, and it was Zoe who deterred him from that. Now it was time to repay part of that loan – he decided. She loved the rockets, so they headed toward the Rocket Museum, located North West from the city.

Aa was amazed to see the crude rockets in their underground chambers to sit and wait for eternity to arrive.

Zoe loved the place; she was practically pulling Aa to show her knowledge on pre-civil war machinery.

"Look, these were the ones that carried the nuclear bombs to the South, to the Land of the Aggressors!" She stopped near a fortified bunker. They all walked up to the rim. Beyond laid six empty tubes in circular pattern.

"You could've destroyed this planet forever!" Aa uttered just loud enough for Zoe to hear. Startled, she turned to her. Aa noticed and corrected herself. "We could've destroyed this beautiful planet, once and for all!"

"But they had only two bombs! One destroyed the naval base, the other exploded prematurely!" She recited the often heard answer.

"Of course she knows only what she understood, not the horrible things war had done to people!" Erin walked up to them, uttering into Aa's ears.

"Papa, can I get some ice cream?" Zoe clung to his father's arm.

"All right, but wait here!" Erin replied and gently patted her daughter's head.

"I'll walk with you!" Aa decided and they left the girl watching the past.

"It's so nice that you found time to be with us today!" Erin said on their way to the kiosk.

"You two have a special place in my heart, you know that!" Aa tried to ease the situation.

"I really meant the things I said up at the rim. I never took her to the radiation sickness displays or the recovery efforts area. I mean the scientists talked after the war was over how much we depleted our natural resources how we lived on the land without consciousness, but never before the war! That we almost destroyed our own world, hence the energy conservation measures at night, the electric cars and subways but I think after the war a new world order came to light. They want all our money. They want us to believe that if we want to survive we must follow them beyond the edge of the horizon; especially if we want our children to live too. Such bullshit if you ask me and I am afraid, Zoe believes them wholeheartedly! I tried to steer her away from that, but I think I failed. She really wants to be a scientist, to help humanity, instead of picking up a useful profession!" Erin finished his speech, agreeing with the ice cream seller on the issue.

"Hold these!" He turned toward Aa and spotted her tears on her beautiful face. He stopped for a second, frowned. "Shit, you believe in it too?"

She shook, wiped off her tears and opened her fingers toward the cold delicate. "I love you so much, such a nice guy, but sometimes you are so wrong!" She took the ice creams so he could grab his.

"Look we're grownups here…" Erin tried to tilt the situation to his favor.

"That doesn't make it any different!" Aa disagreed a bit shaking as the emotions suddenly washed over her.

"I saw things in the war I don't think I should. I told you my father died at the end and I saw him burn to death but what I didn't tell you is that he showed me, thru the windows an arm. It had only five fingers! What kind of sick bastard plays with human evolution? Were they trying to create super humans? Super soldiers? Maybe that's why they give us this load of crap about the old ways and the new. They don't want us to mingle in whatever they figured out! Let me tell you something else! Once the main recovery was over, things settled they wanted to give me an electric car too. I said hell, no! I protested, stood up, and voila, I got an old prewar cruiser! Its big, it's protective and it goes until the gas runs out! No little boxes on three wheels, oh I forgot to charge it overnight crap! I tell you Aa, they want us to believe something that isn't true!" Erin was happy to give the lowdown to someone.

Aa was on the other hand disappointed. She hoped he could change, but now it seemed he was a lost cause, despite all his greatness. She swallowed hard and turned to him, attempting to smile. "Look, let just change the subject! I take the investigation goes well, you even had time to take off to be with us!"

"Actually it isn't. The crazy professor said the intruders were interested in the blueprints of the pre-war and the after war city layout! Why, I don't know!"

"Maybe something was stashed away?" Aa thought loudly.

"What?" Erin stopped.

"Think about it, if what you said is really true and the government was trying to create super soldiers, maybe the whole enemy landing north of the city was an attempt to get their hands on them. Worried that this gets on the wrong hands, so to speak they burnt the place and hid the knowledge somewhere deep in the city. What do you know about the Land of the Aggressors nowadays? Maybe they're sending agents here to retrieve the information and start a war again!" Aa finished it, unsure if ultimately this was a great idea to tell or not.

Erin slowly nodded. "Very interesting. Scary thing and you could be right! I need to contact my government sources to find out more about the Land of the Aggressors myself! Unfortunately this means I can't be with you tomorrow! You're such a great help to me!" Erin kissed her unexpectedly, than bent forward, to give the ice cream to Zoe. "Princess!"

"Should I turn around to give another minute to the grownups?" Zoe asked his father who blushed. Aa giggled and they all licked the ice cream together.

"Did you have to open up Pandora's Box?" Smith rolled his eyes after hearing Aa's story of how her day went.

"I ran my mouth, I admit, but think about it in our context. It could be that they really hid the information somewhere in the city! If the enemy was really close they might destroyed the place to protect the UNHL, but sent the data in one form or the other away!"

Smith spent couple minutes thinking it over then concluded: "You might be onto something! Sorry for my outburst. You're doing a great job while you relaxing as well. I am happy for you more ways than you can think of, however we are running out of time!" Smith concluded the obvious, and then added: "I have to leave to run an errant with the Toxic and I need to do it alone!" He added.

"I'll go with you!" Azure jumped upon hearing the news. She was promptly cooled down by Smith. "I told you, I have to do it alone!" He then turned to Josh. "Arrange a pick up for tonight!"

"Done deal, we'll do it this time outside of the city!"

"I don't care!" Smith gestured with his hands. He was annoyed by the fact that he couldn't get any closer to the solution and it wasn't just a simple case. People will start dying real soon unless he finds what he came here for and eradicating a whole planet will plunge the UNHL into a very real war with the AOCP and in that case he won't be able to save his friends, his people, the citizens who swear an oath to serve him...

Chapter Twenty Four

The accident

Erin met his source from the government who denied any kind of allegation regarding to the creation of super humans, although he acknowledged that the Land of the Aggressors were open for visitors; the government helped rebuild cities there too.

"How come it isn't in the news?" Erin sat shocked.

"Touchy subject... We helped rebuild their infrastructure and rooted out the insurgents, made them peaceful again. Our government spent considerable amount of money to..."

"I am not the right person, but shouldn't the people supposed to know about it?" Erin stopped him in mid-sentence.

"Of course they should know and they will. The President will have a national speech next week, for the fifth anniversary of the first launched satellite. In his speech he'll discuss that the space program is a joint cooperation between the Land of the Aggressors and us. He'll also mention that the borders will be open and that their society survived however the less than ten million survivors that left alive, needs our assistance to survive!"

"There were tens of millions living there before the war!" Erin was taken aback by the source's claims.

"Key word is before. We killed them, crushed their government. Millions died in radiation sickness, they are no more as an independent nation. The president is ironing out a protectorate status for them, because they are un-capable to sustain themselves!"

"This is horrible! Then, they wouldn't have the capability to attack us?"

"That is out of the question although there were rumors that part of their leadership went into hiding along with the military, but we concluded if they did, they had to leave the Southern Islands. We are working around the clock to find them, building a series of military satellites that will be launched as soon as early fall to map the planet, to see underwater. We are very concerned of that near surface underwater anomaly off the East Coast! If the tonight flight will show that it isn't moving we will launch military vessels as early as midnight! As I said, there are possibilities but they aren't coming from the land."

"What about the silent helicopters? Have you ever seen them?" Erin named his curiosity.

"Never saw any of them, but there are rumors in certain government circles that a program might exist to shelter the President from disasters and silent helicopters would be one possible way to do it, but it is nothing more than sheer speculation at this point!"

"Thank you again for your service!"

"I helped your father it's only fair I help you too!" The man said then got into his electric car and zipped away.

Erin was troubled by what he heard, but it seemed it wasn't connected to his hypothetical case at all. He daydreamed about the green helicopters, thinking about what his source had said. There was something he didn't tell, he could feel but couldn't name it what so ever. It seemed that maybe others seen those helicopters too. Because he was daydreaming, he didn't see the tree branch on the road and by the time he realized something was on the road it was too late. He ran over the branch, rocking the car and suddenly it was veering off the road. He had to counter steer hard to keep the car straight and finally stopped. As he got out of the car and walked around he noticed his shaking hands. *What a mess!* His right side rear tire went out; he had a flat. He checked the trunk for a spare and gathered his tools at the gorgeous sunset. He was pissed he didn't bring his aide with him, he was pissed he agreed to this meeting so far away from the city. No phone booths, no help, no traffic. He put out his reflective squares and started to work on the lug nuts.

He was just about to swap the tire when he heard a noise. Another car was coming from the city. He frowned. Who the hell would leave the city at night? This particular road ended at the tip of the island, a natural habitat area and a monument for the landing of the Land of the Aggressors. He checked his gun and popped his back just in time to see another battered car's headlights. The other car slowed down and pulled over. The driver stopped the engine and got out. "Do you need help?"

"Thank you, I messed up my wrench, but this is an older model, don't know if you have one…" Erin stated. It was true. He messed up the wrench with the last lug nuts. It was too tight and now he couldn't remove the nut from it.

"Just a moment!" The other driver said and opened his trunk. After a moment he held up his prize. "I've got it!"

Erin remained suspicious toward the other man, although his voice was familiar from somewhere. As the man approached, he recognized him. "Aren't you the famous Aas from radio PS?"

"That would be me, sir!" The guy offered his hand.

Erin smiled and took it. "The pleasure is mine! I'm a big listener of you, my name is Erin!"

"Ah, the Police Chief! No aide?" Aas frowned.

"Yes, I had something to do alone!" Erin decided not to say too much, to reveal something by accident.

"No doubt looking for those mysterious, green and silent helicopters, right?" Aas smiled and gave a hand fixing up Erin's spare on the car.

Erin was so happy that he practically begged for a picture together with the famous radio host. He had a new digital camera. Zoe told him many times to swap pictures together for good memories, but the prints were too costly so he went for the digital version. Zoe could download the images to a personal computer -he almost never used-, to show to her girlfriends...

Aas had to show him the self-timer and how to use it. He took the picture while arm in arm, his car behind them and he was happy!

*

Smith was finally reeled in to the cabin of the modified Mi-24 AVD and he was on his way toward Josh's SCC to tell him to move about four kilometers to any directions to avoid detection by government airplanes. He spotted two cars on the nearby road and hoped nobody had the idea to look up as the helicopter accelerated away, its silent engine running at maximum.

Chapter Twenty Five

Erin fiddled with the computer at home. Zoe was asleep and he wanted to print out the picture. He wanted to keep one in the car, but couldn't figure out how to use the darn printer. Instead he went for a close up look on the picture after he won the battle how to handle the zoom in and out button. He smiled as he zoomed in his own face '*what a handsome man*!' he smiled, but his heart stopped sort of when he realized the dark spot on the picture, right on his car's rear view mirror. It was undoubtedly...a green helicopter with a person being reeled on or off. He just couldn't tell. A wide smile crossed his face; now he had a proof. He has to take it to Aas tomorrow!

Erin was so busy the next day he practically forgot about the picture. First it was his boss Adams who wanted a morning report, than Mr. Erdmore called in to get a feel of the situation. He promised resources for Erin to gear up the investigation if he needs it. Then it was back to the NSA where he was given proof of the erased markers and what information the intruders were after as a hard copy, but he couldn't really make heads or tails of it. Never less he took the papers back to the station along with a high resolution digital layout of the city. The NSA was so kind they actually marked the buildings that remained intact before and after the war. They marked yellow those whom partially destroyed and the rest remained black against white background. Erin firmly held his belief that Mr. Erdmore pushed them toward cooperation, but instead he ordered Corporal Tok to start looking into the changes, locate the buildings and find out whom were their owners then left for home because he was hungry and he promised a splendid dinner for his girlfriend...

He surveyed the dinner table and found everything perfect, but as Zoe pointed out, the main dish plate was on the wrong side.

"I knew that!" He pressed on his lips and moved the plate to the correct position.

"I should've sent my aide to pick her up!" He concluded.

"Your cruiser is for work, not for pleasure!" Zoe reminded him, and then added to ease his father's anger: "She was living as an independent person for such along while; she would want it that way too!"

Erin kissed her daughter's forehead. She was such a smart and adept person, sometimes he wondered if she might be an angel of some sort...

The bell rang and broke up the moment.

"She is early!" He looked up to the clock, hanging on the wall.

"She probably just as nervous as you are!" Zoe shrugged and walked to the door to open it.

Aa hoped her conservative, but petite black dress will be okay for the occasion. Most of her youth she wore skintight clothes back on Down Earth, jeans and miniskirts after meeting Evan Smith and military uniform onboard her given ship, the Executor. She didn't miss her birthplace, perhaps because she lost everyone close to her early on. She had to make due what she had; natural ability to adapt, to learn and to kill. She used these abilities to get close to Smith, to ask his help to find out about her parents. Her life wasn't the same since... She was a bit nervous to knock on the door of an upscale, but old apartment building, on an alien planet where she supposed to extract crucial information from a man she also loved... It certainly complicated things...

The door opened and Zoe giggled at her. "You are so cute tonight, come on in!"

"Thanks!" Aa replied, walking thru the short hallway, full of old picture frames and a coat hanger. She led her into the second room that once upon a time served as a dining room, next to the kitchen. It was stuffed with older furniture; candles and more pictures. In the corner a vision device stood - a box on four legs. She spotted Erin, who wore a deep grey and black top, grey pants and black shoes. "You're looking sharp!" She kissed him on the cheek.

"...And you are just like an angel in black!" Erin mustered her little bit too long.

"Thank you." Aa hid her blush behind a smile. It was inconvenient to be called by her old nickname, but of course, luckily Erin never believed her, only his daughter... She was called a black angel before; it was her nick name in Delta City where she became a contract killer, rising from the slum...

"I do hope you like our dinner! I was expecting you a bit later, so I have to check on it!" Erin apologized than before he disappeared in the kitchen he instructed his daughter: "Zoe, show her some of the pictures, maybe she want some of it!"

"Sure thing Papa!" She grabbed Aa's hand and pulled her into the first room. It was hers alone! Aa looked on the selves where books stood in long lines. Her toys in the back, but it remained strange to Aa no matter how many times she visited her domain. Zoe turned on the computer; a desk size machine. Actually it was built into the desk itself. She turned around to see what Aa was doing.

"Hey!" She smiled as Aa combed the hair of a baby toy.

"I am sorry, I should've asked first!" Aa placed the toy back to its place on the self.

"No, no, I'm just curious! Most of my girlfriends come to see my library nowadays. As a grownup I expected you find comfort among the books that hold knowledge, since you are so smart yourself!"

As a reaction Aa moved toward the long shelves full of books. She noted again that most of them were scientific books. She frowned as she pulled out one. It had handwritings on it. She recognized as Zoe's.

"I know, I am still a child, I should enjoy it 'til it last!" Zoe told in a deep voice as most of the time the grownups tell her, then added: "You told me this already..."

Aa laughed, bend forward and looked deep into the child's eyes. "You are smarter than most kids, don't waste it, but enjoy that little innocence you have left. Once you became a grownup, there is no more innocence! The world and your decisions will weigh heavy in your shoulders!"

Zoe tried to read into what Aa had said. She was often a mystery to her. A woman of contradictions: so beautiful but not showing herself as such. So smart but not showing herself as such, so handsome yet so raw...

The moment was broken by a ping from the computer. Zoe turned around and walked to the chair and pointed to Aa. "Sit down, miss!" She smiled and showed her the pictures they took at the outdoor museum the other day.

"What's this paper?" She pointed to the desk where numbers were written with Erin's handwriting.

Zoe walked close to the desk and took a peek while frowning. "Homework of sorts…"

"What?"

"Papa must want me to print these for him!"

"Homework, huh?" Aa smiled on her reaction.

"I'll go and ask! Until that, you could use the controls to go to the next picture." She pointed to the joystick on the side.

Aa began to browse them until she came upon the last one. '*Shit*!' She thought when she recognized Aas and Erin against the Chief's car. She zoomed in and noticed the black spot in Erin car's mirror. She used more zoom and was horrified when she made out the MI-24AVD in the car's mirror. She had to do something and quickly!

She turned around to see as Zoe was still going over the printing list with his father and when her head was back she was already learning the controls. Primitive program, but it was intuitive and useful. She didn't want to delete the picture. That would be bad, but maybe… She was happy to find an eraser tool. She set the colors to the background and erased the helicopter. She saved the file and lay back on the chair just in time for Zoe's return.

"Can you help me to turn on the printer?" She asked Aa.

"Sure thing!" She smiled and pushed in the button on the huge square box, the first, mass produced, personal color printer of Agross V.

They figured out how to load up the images to the printer then left to eat dinner. Aa liked the main meal so much, she asked for the recipe.

She had to admit, Erin knew how to cook. The man insisted to take her home, but she previously arranged with Diesel to be picked up by eleven o'clock. They talked about innocent and not so innocent things after Zoe went to sleep: "I don't want to push up on things, but I arranged Zoe to sleep over her friend's house tomorrow. If you think it's appropriate I would like to spend the evening with you!" Erin tested the waters.

"Perhaps the whole night as well?" Aa flashed her perfect smile.

"I would like that!" Erin grinned and kissed her passionately, but broke up once the bell rang.

"Your father!" He jumped up like a kid who did something he not supposed to do... Aa laughed and kissed him one more time before Erin walked her to the door.

Erin went to work the next day, but his mind wondered about his girlfriend. He was still unsure if he could call her as such, so in public he referred to her as a female friend.

Corporal Tok and the aides from the department spent the entire yesterday to come up with something useful regarding the map, but so far they had nothing beyond wild theories such as the one that involved a department store that used to be a slaughter house before the war...

Erin had his own theories and tried to ask the coroner's help to see if he agrees. He did, so Erin was only looking for newly built warehouses. He went as far that he checked out two, promising candidates himself. Of course they turned out to be just as what they were: warehouses. This exercise also landed him front of Rally Adams who wanted to see him as one of the warehouse owner called Erin's visit a harassment.

Erin agreed and agreed again, but just before leaving he got a call from Mr. Erdmore who wanted to speak to him. He reluctantly agreed. He drove the cruiser himself, he wanted to stop by Mrs. Edna to see if Zoe was okay and to thank her to allow her to spend the evening and the night there.

Erin walked into the city's biggest park. It was afternoon. The park was filled by playing kids, young mothers and joggers alike. He sat down on the bench located on the left side of the outer ring around the park; the second one under the light pole and watched the passersby. A tall man in a brown trench coat sat down beside him and when he turned toward the newcomer, he just said: "Keep looking straight, Chief!"

Erin lightly smiled, looking relieved. "I didn't know you were a master of disguise!"

"I am many things!" Mr. Erdmore said, then after a pause he added: "I know about your visits to two sites, I agree with your methods, but this time it's too aggressive. All it takes is one article in the newspaper about cops checking out businesses without proper paperwork and we could lose control over the situation!"

"I beg to disagree; we don't have control over it!" Erin shook his head.

"Point taken!" The turncoat agreed.

"Do you have something to suggest, sir?"

"As a matter of fact I am. I'm certain that a storm is coming unlike anything before!" He sniffed into the air.

Erin frowned.

"Did you ever notice before; you can smell the rain from down the street even though you still walking in the sunshine? …A storm is coming, better get relaxed, because I need you to make that phone call to me when it happens!"

"What phone call?"

"When things getting out of hand… I've positioned some experts near the city. They are on twenty two hours standby, ready for my call."

"Are they military?"

"Special Forces; the best!" Mr. Erdmore added.

"Are you thinking whom we after might turn out to be aliens?" Erin delved further.

"If they are we're in deep trouble. No, this may be the past, haunting us. We've received some evidence from the Land of the Aggressors, now known as Southern Protectorate that suggests of a covert mission to save political, military leaders and their families after the war. They suggesting that these people might be hiding on the other side of the planet, where the Million Islands lie. Needless to say we are very concerned and we're taking steps to make sure it didn't happen, but it may take some time as it's very difficult to get there."

"But you do everything you can, right?" Erin bit his lips. Somebody else's problems just became his…

"Correct. I'm working with the military to arrange a swift and mobile task force guarded by two submarines and some refueling ships and they will leave before the weekend, but I have a bad feeling… The Paranoia Station maybe onto something regarding to the acoustics near the northern tip of the island…"

"I have the feeling that I'm not supposed to know this…" Erin sounded concerned.

"Again, you are correct!"

"Will I disappear without of a trace?" He took a deep breath before asking.

"No. I believe you will be the right man for the right post when the time comes, but of course, don't fuck it up, okay?" He patted his shoulder then left, leaving Erin and his newfound problems behind.

Erin smoked a cigar before walking back to his car. The sun was setting slowly, painting the sky in golden hue. The engine roared lightly as he took off from the parking spot. He was heading toward the northern workers class neighborhood where his daughter was staying overnight.

Mrs. Edna was a nice woman in her late thirties. Her apartment was on the third floor, but of course there was no elevator there and Erin had to stop to catch his breath before he knocked on the door to look fit.

Zoe peaked from behind as soon as Mrs. Edna opened the door. "Papa!"

"Darling, is everything all right?" Erin smiled, but some of the wrinkles from his forehead never disappeared.

Zoe noted his troubles, but decided to ask later.

"Mr. Erin, so nice to come by, care to come in?"

"Oh, no I just wanted to thank you personally to take care of my daughter!"

"No problem, I'll walk them to the bus stop in the morning, and make sure they have their IDs on them for the visit!" Edna replied thoughtfully.

"What visit?" Erin tried to inquire politely.

"Oh, she didn't tell you? The whole class got accepted for the technology fair, held downtown in the Bank of Akron!" Mrs. Edna smiled.

Erin turned to his daughter, who shrugged. "I didn't want to tell you, Papa, I know you are always against technology!"

"Why? Do you have something to do with it?" Erin knew his daughter all too well.

"They sort of liked my essay!" She shrugged again, frowning herself too.

"Your daughter is a little genius!" Mrs. Edna added; patting Zoe's back.

"I see! We'll talk about this later, darling!" Erin added with a hint of a threat in his voice then turned back to Mrs. Edna thanking her kindness one more time before leaving. This time he pre-ordered from a restaurant, but he was working on the soup himself. On the way to pick up the food, he turned on the radio.

"...certainly sir, I think it is great idea! Please call in if you can to support our initiative! If the CDM see how much the citizens are concerned about the hydroponics system's sensitive ears maybe they will launch the Special Task Force ships to investigate, not just sending a military plane in high altitude to search for large objects floating on the waters. After all nobody want to see some nasty and deadly surprise for the weekend! Again this is Aas, host of the PS, your only source of up to date information, the government doesn't want to tell you! I'll be back after the following commercials!"

Erin frowned. Mr. Erdmore was right about it, this could be trouble! Suddenly he remembered the picture he took with Aas earlier this week, and about his discovery of the green helicopter in the car's mirror. He had to remember to that one!

His first reaction was to call in, to agree with Aas, but then he remembered about his delicate case and his 'public image' and decided to shut his mouth. But still, he was excited, couldn't wait for the evening. Of course, his baby will come over... He smiled and made a turn.

Aa just got out of the shower. She surveyed her choices for the evening and decided over some red t-shirt and a tight, washed off jeans. She was just about dressed when Baby came in smiling. "Girl, you are glowing!"

"You think so?" She giggled.

"I am happy for you!" She offered some red lipstick to her before turning around. "Do you think I need makeup?" Aa frowned.

"Girl, you don't need a thing beside a man. I need to go back to the planning room!"

"Why, what's wrong?" Aa frowned again.

"Diesel thinks the host of the PS station is trouble..."

"I told him that from the beginning!" Aa shrugged.

"He believes we have to do something!"

"Josh is in charge, at least that's what Smith said to all of us, so let him figure it out!"

"Kulighan agrees." Baby frowned. "We don't want you to worry yourself! We'll take care of this problem while you have fun with your alibi." Baby Haas said from the doorway before disappearing.

Aa thought about it for a moment than decided that Diesel was right; Aas has to be neutralized. She was hoping it will not be a permanent one, knowing Diesel that was a real possibility... She checked herself in the mirror and decided to grab a white light coat against the evening wind. She imitated a kiss toward the mirror. "Come and lick me!" She grinned then left.

"You are looking great!" Erin said, peeking over to Aa who sat beside him in the police cruiser.

"You told me that twice already!" She smiled warmly.

"Well, then I just going to tell you one more time!" He agreed with himself and turned on the radio.

"...Ladies and gentlemen, the lines are flooded with calls from phone booths, form work, from bars and the citizens are all demanding the CDM to launch an immediate investigation into the case of the water readings. My informant acknowledged that the ministry is concerned, however they think my little show is nothing to be considered with. Let us show that they are wrong, listen to me tomorrow morning at six am and I shall lead us to redemption! The ministry is taxpayer funded; we shall have our right to be considered serious! This is again Aas at the PS!"

"Don't you think he has gone overboard?" Aa turned to Erin.

Erin turned down the radio as he replied. "I really don't see why the CDM can't check that out on sea. They keep giving that formal bullshit about sending an airplane but since they don't see anything they don't think it's there. I say, what if it's deep underwater, like a sub or something?" Erin shrugged. "What's your opinion on it?"

"I have no opinion!" Aa brushed him off, but he wanted some kind of answer out of her, so he pressed on.

"You are of course right, something isn't right, but maybe it's just a glitch in the software! I rather believe in my eye before anything!" Aa replied after careful consideration.

"Oh, come on Aa don't you try to tell me you aren't curious about it!"

"I am not!" She lied, shaking her head.

"Strange, I would've thought it otherwise. You seemed good with that computer stuff!"

"...Hence why I say that they should check the programming before causing rampant paranoia and turning this small problem into a wide scale civil unrest! I mean you were there too, at the NSA. They screwed up the recovery effort, they are probably the ones whom behind this too!"

"You right!" Erin grimaced, while cooling off. She was right. They most likely contracted the NSA to this and they are making mistakes, after all Mr. Erdmore knew they were being hacked or something before the NSA came to that conclusion themselves...

He took a deep breath and sent the matter to a deep corner in his mind while concentrated in something much more pleasurable nearby.

Chapter Twenty Six

Kidnapping

Aas was up earlier than usual; he wanted to live up to his promise and launch a picketing line front of the CDM by the time the rush hour starts so he took the first bus to the radio station. It was still dark, but the stars were disappearing: dawn was coming...

He walked past some of the parking cars. He would've came with his own, but decided against it. Nobody needs to know his license ID or that he has an old styled car. He was trying to predict his morning, how exactly is he going to raise the people's attention when suddenly a short, brown haired girl appeared seemingly out of nowhere. She flashed her smile and he was thrown off of his track.

"Can I help you miss?" He frowned.

"As a matter of fact, you can!" It was something in her sweet voice that threw off the switch in his brain, but before he could get his ideas in motion, somebody hit him on the back of his head and all the light went out; he fell to the ground.

The first thing he realized was that his head hurt like hell, worse than when he was on drugs...

The second thing he noticed that it was still dark because he was blindfolded...

He heard people around him talking in a language he never heard before, and then they walked farther, no doubt to discuss his miserable life and dim future.

His hands were tied behind a chair he was sitting on.

His mouth was gagged.

He panicked; he was kidnapped!

He tried, but couldn't even move a muscle…

Couple minutes later, he heard the noise of a distant door being opened then closed. Somebody walked in. It was a heavy door on old hinges. A newcomer arrived Aas figured. He heard the same unknown language. The male voice hollered something short, and then a door to his left opened. Somebody else walked in into his room along with the newcomer.

He heard a voice, with a strange accent he never heard before: "I abducted him!" The male voice sounded proud.

"Why?"

Aas listened carefully. He was good at remembering voices. He heard this one before, but couldn't quite put it when and where.

"He was really annoying!" The first voice replied.

"I told you, no abductions!" The second voice was full of anger.

"Let me talk to you on the side!" The first voice said then Diesel pulled Smith aside.

"Where is Aa?" Smith was missing her from his count and it annoyed him a bit. He wondered if Mr. Erin was behind her sudden disappearance. Waste of time, he thought with more and more anger, but then he realized the only thing he was doing was fooling himself; he was jealous of him! It should've been him who is with her like that. It could've been like that at one point of their life, before Azure and he didn't take it. Now he saw what he was missing out on. She wasn't just pretty, hot and sexy but loyal as well. Something he was longing for a long time in a neat package like Aa…

Diesel was highly annoyed by the radio host and he felt happy to abduct him, so now he was standing proudly behind his own actions: "Aas was planning a rally today to pressure the Interior Ministry to send warships and bombard the East Coast waterline! We can't communicate with the ship right now. Not until the afternoon. He announced this yesterday and their listeners initial response was demanding the President himself to get to the bottom of this! We had to act. He'll be unharmed. We will be long gone before he is found and after that, well it isn't our concern then!"

"All right but where is Aa?" Smith hugged Azure and acknowledged Baby's presence.

"She spent the evening and night with Erin!" Josh walked away from the prisoner.

Smith rolled his eyes, than pointed to Diesel. "Get the car!" He then turned to Baby. "Are we packed yet?"

"Yes!"

"Good! Evacuate this place! I'll have a word with him!" Smith walked toward Aas. He loudly asked from the gagged man: "Do you remember my voice?"

Aas nodded. The now familiar voice removed the ball from his mouth so he could answer, but not his blindfold. He replied licking his dry lips. "Yes."

"You are here because you annoy me and because you interfere with my plans!"

"To enslave us, no doubt!" Aas replied with a sinister voice.

"If that was my plan, you would be slaves by now! This isn't how it works. I'm not that kind! However, You stand in my way. You will not be harmed and when my job is over, you'll be released, I promise!" The familiar voice continued. It was from the park from last week: the man who put the spell on him. He had to be, Aas was certain, but he hollered never less.

"Liar!"

"You'll see!" Smith waved for Josh, to put the guy's gag back on then he was about to signal his team to leave when the apartment's phone rang. Diesel picked up, frowned on whoever was on the other side then held it up high, so Smith could see. "It's for you!"

Chapter Twenty Seven

Erin concluded he had the most wonderful night in a long time. He woke up with dawn and watched the delicate body breathing beside him. Her chest periodically moved up and down; all the rage and the lust, the joy and the sadness were behind them now. He moved her hair aside, to admire the most beautiful face in this world he came to know. He was in love from day one and he was sure she was the right one for him and for Zoe too. He wanted to tell that to her and his thoughts drew smile on his face as he went to the kitchen to make breakfast for both of them.

She just woke up when he returned. Aa smiled at him with a certain warmth. She sat up and let the rolling covers expose her upper body. She giggled as she watched Erin kiss her chest then kiss her.

"Here is your breakfast, princess!" He smiled and brought the plate to her lap.

"I'll turn up wider then taller if you keep up the good work!" She took a bite. It was delicious.

"I think we are made for each other!" He watched her eating. He spotted some clouds on her face, but she didn't reply. He opened his mouth to add something, but she shook her head. "Please, don't ruin this perfect moment! I want to remember to this to the rest of my life!" She touched his bare chest.

After breakfast they took a shower together. Aa just finished dressing up when Erin's beeper went off. Erin took a peek at the display and scoffed at the number. "My boss!" Suddenly the house phone rang too.

Aa frowned. What a commotion early in the morning!

Erin picked up the phone and Aa knew at an instant something was wrong.

He went pale.

Something was very wrong!

"Yes, sir, I am on my way, sir!" He said into the phone, than hung up. "I can't take you home; there is a situation at the First bank of Akron."

"I'll go with you!" Aa said while thinking if this had anything to do with her case.

"I don't think it's safe!" He shook his head then watched her face became contorted. "What's wrong?"

"Your daughter is there!" She said with horror; her hand shaking.

"What?!"

"Remember, today was her class's trip there!" Aa of course knew, Zoe told her the day before. She was so proud, her teachers were so proud that she won first prize in her district. A paper that was called for modernization… All not important things now…

"Oh no!" Erin went paler. He inhaled deeply to force oxygen into his brain and grabbed the door handle.

"I'm going with you!" She demanded and helped him lock the door behind as they stormed out of the building.

Aa was involved in hostage situations or with places she had to storm in before, but she never before had to deal with her own feelings. She was never attached to one of the hostages and now she avidly analyzed her own emotions. It was frightening, she realized. Smith had to have hard time whenever he sent friends to fight - she understood that now. She was sitting on a chair, inside the mobile police headquarters. The police worked hard to keep away the reporters and the bystanders while setting up a tight cordon around the block. One police helicopter hovered above then flew away, but not too far; she was sure. As soon as they arrived she grabbed Erin's cruiser's phone and dialed Diesel. She felt somewhat relieved when she found out that Smith had in fact returned. At the same time she was nervous; not just because her loved ones were involved but because Smith sounded angry and that had to have long term consequences. However, in this case she felt to be the mother and her adopted 'children' was in trouble. All she had to do is watch Erin's face to get reassurances of the situation's seriousness. He had a minor nervous breakdown, before he tried to volunteer to be swapped. Aa was standing by him at the van's open door, looking into the crowd, trying to spot Evan Smith.

"Listen to me, it will be all right!" Aa held his face in her soft palm, trying to make an eye contact with him.
"What the hell is going on here?" She suddenly heard a familiar voice.
"Smith, you've got to help me!" She turned around.
Smith was towering nearby. He was pissed, she could tell.
"While I don't deny, your unusual method was helpful to a point we not supposed to get involved here, especially not emotionally!" He added scoldingly.
"Are you disappointed?" She questioned him in the open.
"Of course I am! Beside the fact that you'll going to hurt him later you'll hurt yourself emotionally too! I don't want to see you hurt, we have a job to do here, remember?"
"Smith, I just found out last night, this is the only known, working bank that was a bank before and during the civil war!"

"Is this helpful, how?" Smith blinked.

"The blueprints, what the AOCP is after?" She hinted.

Smith blinked at them again.

Erin was confused. He drank some water from a bottle. Aa's brother seemed to take charge and his girlfriend wanted that way, he wondered why?

The man turned around and something of how he moved made Erin cautious. When the man turned back he was serious. "You're correct Aa! Evil minds are inside, working on their sinister plan that cares nothing about the hostages! Josh, contact Tarbuk!" He turned to the man Erin knew as half-brother of Diesel.

"We don't want to break radio silence!" Josh reminded him.

Erin wondered about that statement too. What it meant? Maybe they are working for Mr. Erdmore? It would make sense to keep an eye on him, but he was unsure, maybe his own paranoia was taking over...

Smith was fuming: "I don't care about it now! Call and tell him to scan for cloaked objects. He'll find the Toxic if he is good! Have him draw a loose blockade and stop any ship at any cost!"

"Yes sir!" Josh walked away.

"What is the Toxic? What are you talking about and who are you people?" Erin shook his head. He was losing it. Maybe they were Mr. Erdmore's agents after all...

"Smith, help us!" Aa pleaded while she grabbed Smith's shoulder.

"What?"

"Since I've met you I never asked anything besides recovering my past, now I ask this one! Save his daughter for me!"

"Help them!" Smith's girlfriend walked up to him, putting her soft hand on his arm. Erin was totally confused, but listened as the girl he once described as a 'sex-toy' gave a lowdown of the situation she saw and it purely shocked him. She said: "If kids like Zoe be allowed to live, they will propel this culture to the stars, where they belong. In five hundred years they could be part of us! If people like Erin remain in control they will die here in this planet!"

Aa's brother flinched. Erin watched his emotions battle on the surface. He seemed to be weighting on something - Erin had no clue what that was. Then to his biggest surprise the girl added: "Help my girlfriend to save hers!" She pleaded.

Aa's brother closed his eyes and Erin knew he lost. There were powerful women around them...

He heard a gun's 'clack'. He turned to the sound's direction and spotted Aa's father, Diesel. He double checked his gun...

Aa's brother turned to Erin. "We need police uniforms to get inside!"

Erin mumbled: "But, I can't..."

"Erin! Do you want to see your daughter alive?" The man was serious.

"Of course, but..." Erin had his doubts. After all these people supposed to be civilians...

"The uniforms then!" Smith demanded and then turned to Diesel: "Guns! Lots of guns and real bullets! Personal gravity shields and do you have the EMP in the trunk?"

"Yes!"

"Arm it! I still have to make sure we aren't exposed unnecessarily!"

"Thank you!" Aa wiped her tears off. Her emotions were real after all. Erin wanted to hug her for that, to cry with her, but of course he couldn't.

"With every help from the Emperor, there is a price to pay, later!" The brother warned her.

"I understood!" She nodded quietly, her eyes watching the ground. She couldn't look into Smith's eyes. Not now.

"No you don't! But you will in twenty one year's Agross time! You'll be here to visit the famed scientist on the planet's first space station!"

"What?" Aa was lost and confused.

"Remember! I came here to spy on minds, I'm primed. I can see the possibilities unfold. If Zoe is saved it will happen!"

"Yes, I will!" Aa nodded and took a gun from Diesel. She checked it with high routine. She aimed to feel its weight, and then put it away. "This will be great for me!"

Erin quietly sat in his car. He didn't understand a word. Things were upside down, inside out. He felt he was moving away from his life, from his girlfriend who spoke in par with his alleged brother. He was sure now that wasn't the case. He was wondering if Aa played herself for him or not. She certainly lied to him, but she was also concerned about Zoe's safety that was obvious. Her 'brother' brought him back from his thoughts.

"Yo! I need you to get all your equipment at least two city blocks away from here!" Smith patted Erin's shoulder.

"What? Why?" He looked up to the man.

"The EMP will make all electronic equipment useless!"

"Why?" He had no idea what was going on.

"To create a diversion!" Smith lied to him. He hoped he'll forget any words he might heard around them.

Erin ordered his aide to move the cruiser out of the area then he returned to the police van, parked nearby. As they climbed into it, they could see the news vans at the next corner, just behind the police cordon.

As Smith switched clothes, he noticed Erin checking his hoisters. He turned to the police Chief. "No! You will stay behind!"

"Why?"

"Deniability!" He then added after a moment of thinking: "You're a good man... We need you outside! You can't get involved!"

"Sir, I am the police Chief I..."

"Your daughter is inside! You are emotionally unsound! You have been compromised. Stay outside and watch!"

"What if they try to kill you?"

"Look into my eyes, deep!" Smith ordered him. Erin moved closer, mustered Smith's face, and then looked away. "You've killed before!" He was shocked.

"Exactly, so as everybody on my team; like Aa, otherwise she would not be with me! I should grab the moment and thank you for helping her relax. I was trying for so long I thought she could never let it go, always the fighter!" Smith turned around to check on his team. They were ready.

Another cop came to the back; he was talking to Erin. He looked mad for some reason.

"What's wrong?" Smith frowned.

"The Civil Defense Ministry sent a truckload of agents. They arrived five minutes ago. I'm relieved from this case until they finished as per the head of the CDM!"

"All the more reasons to withdrawn!" Smith warned him and then ran outside, leaving him in the van.

Erin did as he was told and remained at the police van's doorstep. This whole new development made no sense and Aa haven't said a word to him either before leaving with Smith. It was obvious now, Smith wasn't her brother, neither Diesel her father. Who these people were remained a mystery to him.

Suddenly one of the news van exploded in a great fireball, then all the lights went out, the idling cars cut off, a news chopper above them lost engines and smashed into one of the nearby buildings.

He understood at once what that EMP supposed to do and with that in mind he ran to the nearest bunch of confused cops to help ease the situation and send them to the building the news helicopter crashed in to evacuate. He turned around, but Aa and the rest of her friends were gone. He saw the bank's glass door closing and hoped they made it inside.

Aa tried to concentrate on the task ahead and not to Erin who no doubt is hurt by her show of true colors. Smith was right… She hurt him and it was her own fault, but she could think of that later, once they were done with the bank and with this mission. The most pressing thing for her was to cover for her team mates and to be on the lookout for the hostages, including Zoe! She heard the order from Diesel to switch to laser guns; a sure sign of a serious situation. She switched clips and activated the laser sensor, then aimed as she covered Baby Haas while she jumped in the air, propelling herself across the vault's opening; her guns aimed at waist high. She pulled the triggers as she shot by, landing unharmed on the other side.

As Azure killed two retreating AOCP agents at point blank and informed everybody that the vault is theirs, Aa told Smith that the old vault lies in the same space as the new. She learned that from Erin, inside the police van, when he tried to assess the situation.

Once inside the vault Smith looked around and immediately noticed the huge box on the ground. Some papers were left in the bottom of it. They were written in AED (Ancient Earth Dialect), the old language of the UNHL. He was excited as he read some of the technical manuals. He was on the right track! Unfortunately the precious content of the box was gone... They were obviously pinned down by the rest of the AOCP agents so the others with the real prize can escape!

He grabbed the papers then looked at the five fingered agent, dead on the floor and made a quick mental call for the Toxic. He addressed his crew: "Azure and Gabriel!"
"Yes?" Two heads popped out from the smoke.
"Collect all the agents, take them to the roof, the Toxic is coming! Priority to clean up!"
Nobody had a problem with that since Azure was as strong as any man in the team.

Chapter Twenty Eight

Diesel dived into the smoke and Smith followed him closely. The tunnel ended at the back of the building where tire marks showed that something was there recently. They found some of the hostages at the corner. They were in a state of shock. Aa spotted Greeta all curled up, covering some of her classmates with her body.

She kneeled down and pulled up her mask to talk. Greeta gazed into Aa, faintly recognizing the woman.

"Where is she?" Aa asked.

"They took her!" Greeta was crying.

"Don't worry; I'll take care of it!" She winked to reassure her.

Aa turned around, just in time to see Smith gone ballistic. "Diesel, Aa run to Erin. Get him and the cruiser and our car! Go!" He looked around to see a trash compactor. He cautiously approached the door and opened it. He took a step back even though he expected dead people in it. These were the Civil Defense Ministry's agents. Shot on their head and disposed quickly to make it harder to figure out their next moves...

Erin managed to stabilize the situation and called for the Commissioner to send in more officers when somebody grabbed his arm, hard. He was about to reprimand the person when he realized it was Aa. Her borrowed police uniform was full of cuts and blood, her cute face dusty and sweaty, her hair in disarray. Before he could manage to say anything she yelled with strange excitement in her voice: "They're gone and they took Zoe with them!"

"What are we going to do now?" Erin asked. He couldn't think straight anymore.

"Smith knows, we need to pursue them! Where is the cruiser?"

"This way!" Erin pointed beyond the block as he hollered at Corporal Tok. "Make a hole, coming thru! Tok, take over!"

Squeaking tires woke Smith from his daydreaming. He ran outside just in time to see the nervous Erin backing up his cruiser thru the open gates.

"Time to go!" Smith propelled forward and while Aa took the seat beside Erin, Baby jumped in with him into the back of the car.

"Where to?" Erin asked, not even turning his head.

"Away from the city. Can you get a fix on the CDM's van?" Smith asked.

"Why?"

"Cause they escaped with it!" Smith replied angry. He checked himself and he was not hurt. He emptied the guns and mounted the next clip.

Erin turned to Aa, who touched his hand reassuringly. "It will be okay!" He felt powerful just from the slight touch of her fingers! Instead of calling his boss, he called Mr. Erdmore's private number.

"Chief, what is going on there? Why have you left your post?"

"No time to explain, I need to track your special team's van!" Erin shouted into the phone as he also tried to navigate the car in the city traffic.

"All right, keep the connection, I'll check on it!" Mr. Erdmore said awful calm for Erin's taste. While it seemed it took him forever to get back, in reality it was only thirty seconds. His voice sounded like a man unsure of himself. "Strange! They are moving fast, toward the road that ends on the top of the hills, on the beach north of the island! Are you going to tell me what's going on?"

"All you need to know is to hold your horses, I'm in pursuit!" Erin slammed the phone and grabbed the steering wheel.

"Is this the same road you and Aas ran into each other?" Smith asked.

"How do you know about it?" Erin jaw's dropped.

"Is it?" Smith pressed on.

"No! This splits off on the left. It ends in a park!" Erin shook his head. How did he learn about his trip? Then he realized Aa must've told him when he told it to her. She sold him out!

"Go there the fastest way!" Smith ordered him, and then turned to the girls. "This will be the showdown! I remind you all what's at stake! We need the retro at any cost!"

"Understood!" Aa replied, sadness in her eyes. Erin noted that from where he sat. Whatever this 'retro' was they were here for that. It became obvious for him that they were after the same thing the unknown men were after whom killed without thinking. He hoped he can allow himself a leap of faith and declare; this team was the nicer one. It meant his investigation would end soon, however, he wanted to live, preferably with his daughter. It seemed these people all placed too much faith into Zoe, from Aa to Smith… And while at it, that nonsense about the future was truly out of a Sci-fi movie!

Smith seriously weighed their possibilities, "If we can, we'll delegate! I go for what I need, you go for what you need!"

Aa brightened upon hearing that and kissed his cheek by leaning back.

"Are you going to tell me what is this all about?" Erin managed to ask Aa.

"I am so sorry for all this, that I put you into this position, but I love you still and I love Zoe too! Just watch us and don't get involved!" She added, tears freely running down on her beautiful cheek.

Erin couldn't say anything to that. He drove up the hill; straight into the parking lot, where the CDM van parked abandoned. The doors were open; just one bleeding hostage remained inside. Erin stabilized the boy's wound then ran after Smith and the others. He saw something running thru the woods, running faster than any human, still holding onto some of the hostages, carrying them like bags of sand!

Mr. Smith aimed at the last one and pulled the trigger. The man fell to the grassy ground, still holding the kid. Smith ran past them, not even looking down.

Erin realized it was his job to check the lost hostages and pull them into safety. It was also a convenient way to keep him out of trouble or to see and hear things he not supposed to.

Smith had to get the leader, the person who had what he needed the most.

Aa ran right behind him. She was barely sweating, breathing correctly, ordering her tight muscles to propel her forward at admirable speeds.

Suddenly they arrived to an opening; a beachhead. Two men lay on the ground; apparently Baby already took care of them.

The man on the edge of the opening held up a girl with his right hand, the data crystal in his left.

"Clever, Emperor, but you must retreat or she'll die!" He laughed toward him.

Aa recognized the last hostage as Zoe. She was on her own! Smith wasted no time and jumped forward, going for the crystal.

The AOCP agent was still laughing as he jumped off the ledge, backward, holding the girl and the crystal.

Smith used his gun in midair to severe the agent's hand and grab the bloody end that still held the data crystal. Diesel saw all that and went after Smith, since he was almost beyond the edge.

Aa was in the air as well, dropping into the dirt hard and opening her arm to catch the girl, who screamed.

 Zoe grabbed Aa's arm and held onto it tight as she carefully reeled her back.

On the ground she stood her up. Zoe was petrified, blinking hard at her.

"What's wrong little princess?" Aa moved aside her blonde hair and wiped off her face.

Zoe slowly raised her hand. It held a plastic finger. Aa's sixth finger…

"Don't be scared, you already knew that!" She dropped a lone tear and kissed her forehead as Zoe carefully placed the plastic, yet realistic finger into her pocket.

"Grab the other AOCP agents!" Smith shouted toward the general direction of Diesel and Josh, after thanking them how they saved his life.
"Toxic?" Diesel asked in return.
"She is on her way!"
"Erin is coming!" Josh pointed toward the woods where the Chief's head just appeared.
"I'll deal with him!" Smith moved forward.

Aa wiped of Zoe's face with a napkin and kissed her cheeks. "I'll miss you so much but please remember something sweetheart, for me, okay?"
The scared girl optimistically nodded.
"Seek for the future above the sky; the truth lies beyond the stars! Now, go see your Papa!" She pushed her forward.
Erin closed his arms tight around Zoe as they hugged for a good minute. Smith remained close by as the others brought the dead agents to the edge.
"Can you bring the car up?" Smith turned to Diesel, who shook his head.
"Then get rid of it!"

Erin walked to Aa and he looked into her eyes. "I assume we never see each other again?" He was sad. He finally understood: separation was coming next.
"Never know!" Aa chuckled. She was in tears.
"Who are you anyway?" Erin took a step back. He saw what Smith told him in the city. She was a warrior as she

stood on the beachhead, defiant, bleeding from her arm, yet defending herself and her crew at all cost. He will always remember her that way too, not just the delicate body she allowed him to see, to touch, to kiss, to caress…

"I told you before, you would get disappointed, but what we had, our relationship, I meant it with all my heart! I'll miss you so much!" She kissed him long and passionately.

Smith bent forward, down to the girl's face, "so I guess you're the famous Zoe!" Zoe heard her name to be spoken. It belonged to Smith, Aa's brother. She watched him smile a bit as he kneeled down to the grassy sand.

"You are Smith, her brother, maybe!" She replied, not afraid anymore. These people will not harm her.

"I don't think so!" Smith shook his head; sad and happy at the same time.

"I knew that!" She smiled reassuringly.

"I heard you will going to be a scientist!" Smith continued.

"Maybe? Maybe I'll be a mother, meeting a good man and raising a family!" Zoe replied thoughtfully.

"You know what?" Smith opened her palm to read it.

"What?" She asked in return.

"Maybe you'll be both! Follow the path life has given and you'll be famous and respected!" He flashed his warm smile at her.

"Are you really a fortune teller?"

"I am more than that, but…" Smith looked into her mind. She was such a smart girl for her age. "…you already know that!" Smith stood up, glancing at Aa, signaling her to say good bye to Erin and Zoe.

"Now I have to disobey my teachings, my job and I have to let the bank robbery's accomplices go!" Erin offered his hand to Smith, who took it.

"Look at the bright side: you are alive and so as Zoe. Not to mention of a bunch of hostages. You'll have to take care of this mess, but I'll take the agents with myself. All you have to do is walk away and don't look back! I mean this one!"

"I believe you!" Erin nodded. He not just believed he knew it.

"Oh couple more things!" Smith remembered. "Where we lived in the city, the apartment, on the street is a motorcycle. Here are the keys for it. I am not a good rider, but Aa would be. One more thing! There is a man tied to a chair and gagged in the room. Please rescue him. I told him I am sorry that we held him hostage but he was a really annoying media person!"

"What?" Erin shook his head, not wanting to believe what he just heard with his own ears.

"Go now, our ride is here!" Smith felt the wind as the Toxic arrived under a visibility cloak. He watched the girl and her father leaving the ground then turned around. "Evacuate!"

Diesel appeared shortly, running from all the way from the parking lot where he rigged their car to blow. He was hauling two dead agents, straight up on the hill, nodding toward Erin and Zoe as he passed them.

Erin wanted to turn around, but Zoe hardened her grip on his father's hand. "Papa, don't look back, please!"

"Are you all right my darling?" He looked at his daughter.

"I will be, Papa!"

Chapter Twenty Nine

21 years later, Agross time.

"This is chief scientist Zoe Alberda, to Mission Control in Star City, do you read?" Zoe wore her head set, enjoying the moment while levitating in the rather small space station module.

"This is Greeta Hey from mission control! It's nice to hear your voice Zoe!" She heard her old time girlfriend's call.

"This is Erdmore Evin, Administrator of Star City!" Zoe heard her boss's voice. She smiled and replied: "Nice to hear your voice boss!"

"Same here Zoe. In the name of the Republic and the Southern Province, I give you command to begin the science test aboard our first space station!" He said ceremoniously.

"Ay-Ay!" Zoe replied and maneuvered around a floating crewmember; the other female of the three scientists aboard.

She looked thru the thick, glass, porthole and grabbed the small cylindrical object on a chain around her neck. She just had to touch it!

"Is that a good luck talisman?" Kel asked. He was the mission specialist.

"Something like it! It is from somebody who once saved my life! I wouldn't be here if not for her!" Zoe opened the cylinder and removed a realistic looking plastic finger from it. She kissed then flipped couple switches before placing the cylinder back around her neck, uttering: "I'll find you Aa!"

"This is Greeta from Mission Control, confirming that the tests began. So what do you say, let's make that phone call, shall we?"

"I am ready, call him!" Zoe was full of smiles.

*

"Honey, come on, they already started the live stream!" The woman hollered toward the kitchen where a man in his late fifties grabbed a fine wine and some cookies for the grandchildren. He walked back to the room, gave the cookies to the twin girls and sat down in front of the vision set. He kissed his wife, and then said: "My darlings!"

Suddenly the phone rang.

"Who the hell is it now?" The man frowned and pushed himself up from the armchair.

He picked up the phone and he spoke into it rather annoyingly. "This is police Commissioner Erin Megna, who is this?"

"Papa! I told you I would call you from space!"

*

Prologue

"Admiral on the bridge!" The soldier saluted at the wide bridge's entrance. A tall woman walked thorough. Her heels knocked loudly on the meticulously cleaned floor.

"At ease!" She told them than walked to the radio communications officer. She handed a small, folded paper to the specialist. "I want you to digitize this picture and be ready to send it at my command!"

"Yes Admiral!" The soldier responded while took the paper.

"Emperor is on the bridge!" They all heard it from the Honor Guards stationed at the door. The entire bridge crew jumped up from their stations to salute to the man they served for life.

"At ease!" The man walked past them, headed toward the Admiral.

She turned to him. "Thank you!"

"We'll talk to her together!" He reassured her as he put up a headset for the occasion.

"Begin transmitting our lowest level of protocols toward the object!" The Admiral.

*

Zoe was enjoying her first sleeping period aboard the space station. It took them three years to assemble the T section in space and sent the maiden crew aboard. Suddenly Kel woke her up, he sounded alarmed.

"What's wrong?" Zoe tried to turn, but in space it just didn't work out in such a way.

"We're receiving a radio signal!"

"Take a message!" She snorted.

"Get up Zoe Alberda!" Kel grabbed her arm and began to pull her away from the sleeping tube.

While Zoe didn't like to be dragged, she had to admit it was strange to get a signal, especially when they realized that it was a high frequency, short distance occurrence.

Zoe frowned as she tried to decipher the binary code.

"You think it's the military?" Kel seemed worried.

"Maybe… But then why are they sending this over and over?" She looked at her display. She fiddled with it for a moment, then after an 'aha' moment she compiled the program and ran it on an isolated terminal.

"What is that?" Kel tried to peek over her shoulder.

"Strange, this is a picture viewer!" She shook her head, making her body move too. It was bizarre, never the less she responded toward the general area she believed the signal was coming from with an acknowledging ping. Soon another transmission arrived, this one was more robust and seemed garbage until Zoe realized she could port it into the new program she received. She did, and then as the computer began to draw lines after lines in color, she let out a faint scream. "My Lord, she is here!"

"Who?" Kel frowned. The space station's radar picked up nothing.

"Aa, she came!" Her tears were flowing then levitating away inside the station. She touched her talisman and she felt joy washing over herself.

*

It took a while for Zoe to fall back asleep. She was dreaming, and then all of a sudden she was sitting in a chair, on the beach, facing Aa.

"Am I dreaming?" She asked in her dream.

"No. Smith made it possible to connect our mind!" Aa replied, while smiling.

"Is he the Lord?"

"No, he is just a great leader." Aa laughed, then added, "he is good with minds, he is a telepath."

"I knew he was strange!" Zoe nodded and then looked around. "Can we have a drink? I'm thirsty!"

"Certainly young explorer!" Smith appeared out of thin air and served two drinks, then disappeared.

"None of this is real!" Zoe frowned.

"His mind is connecting us, so I can have this conversation with you, without a trace! Your race isn't that advanced yet to understand us, to walk with us among the stars!"

"Yet you are here!" Zoe disagreed.

"I was always here!" Aa replied, shocking Zoe.

"I don't get it!" She finally replied.

"I am watching over you. When your twins grow up, I'll watch over them too. If I won't be around, then somebody else will!" Aa promised. "Whenever I was sent to the neighboring solar system, I always took the time to sneak around and I always will!"

"Is there something special around here?"

"No, Smith has some properties there. This is actually one of the farthest corners of the galaxy I ever visited!"

"You've been around this galaxy?" Zoe thought she was hallucinating in her own dream.

"The warship I serve on can travel faster than light, but it still takes months to sail across!" Aa let out a sad smile.

"What is your spaceship's name?" Zoe was intrigued.

"I have to go now." Aa glanced up, then added: "Just as in life: Destination Unknown!"

Made in the USA
Middletown, DE
15 February 2020

84826097R00120